And the television . . .

She could not bear to have it on. All that talk. All those experts. All those retired generals and admirals. Their emotionless, unmoving mannequin faces. Lips that hardly moved discussing the chances of death and destruction.

The television had no subject except war.

Nothing mattered but Desert Shield, the generals, the soldiers, the president . . . and Saddam Hussein.

But she could not bear to have the television off, either. Because if she turned it off, something might happen. War might begin. Peace might be arranged. Bombs might drop. The 333rd might be ordered to Saudi Arabia.

Other Bantam Starfire Books you will enjoy

OPERATION: HOMEFRONT

Caroline B. Cooney

BANTAM BOOKS
NEW YORK · TORONTO · LONDON · SYDNEY · AUCKLAND

RL 5, age 10 and up

OPERATION: HOMEFRONT

A Bantam Book/September 1992

*The Starfire logo is a registered trademark of Bantam Books,
a division of Bantam Doubleday Dell Publishing Group, Inc.
Registered in U.S. Patent and Trademark Office and elsewhere.*

ISBN 0-553-29685-X

Published simultaneously in the United States and Canada

Bantam Books are published by Bantam Books, a division of Bantam
Doubleday Dell Publishing Group, Inc. Its trademark, consisting of the
words "Bantam Books" and the portrayal of a rooster, is Registered in
U.S. Patent and Trademark Office and in other countries. Marca
Registrada. Bantam Books, 666 Fifth Avenue, New York, New York
10103.

PRINTED IN THE UNITED STATES OF AMERICA

RAD   0   9   8   7   6   5   4   3   2   1

OPERATION: HOMEFRONT

CHAPTER ONE

Langan was fourteen and not big or tall for his age. His name, which had just been a name until last year, was now a terrible liability. It turned out that people (meaning other boys) thought it was gay. Dealing with the name was a nightmare but Langan said nothing to his parents. What were they supposed to do: rename him Eric?

If he had chosen to stay at the regular high school he'd probably have been okay. Those kids were used to his name, and names you were used to, you didn't make a big deal about. But he'd chosen to go to the county vocational high school, a big, inner-city, racially mixed crowd of far more boys than girls, all of whom found the name

Langan a good enough reason to beat him up. Life in a sweet sheltered suburb had not prepared him for this.

The kids at Washington Vocational High divided into three groups. The ones who did the beating up—he wasn't among them. The kids who got beaten up—he hoped not to be among them. And finally, the kids who stood real still and tried not to be either.

That was him.

Now he understood what it meant to keep a low profile, to keep your nose clean. It meant you didn't get in a fight because you knew you'd lose.

Langan's hero was a kid also in ninth grade, a scrawny black kid whose last name was Astle. It took very little rearranging to come up with Asshole, which was what everybody, including the teachers, accidentally or on purpose, called Astle. Once. Nobody did it twice. Astle took nothing from nobody. Langan didn't know how he did it. Astle had a perfectly good first name—Jerome—which he didn't use; he made everybody use his last name, and he made them say it right. Even the seniors, who were apt to be very muscular after four years of carrying a machine-tool case around all day, didn't bother Astle.

They were too busy bothering Langan.

The one bright spot in adjusting to Washington

Vocational was the outbreak of the Persian Gulf situation.

It was as if the student body and the teachers at Wash had been looking all their lives for something to rally around and now it had happened—a possible desert war.

Each day, the principal gave a five-minute talk on in-school TV about what was happening. Places like Kuwait and Baghdad, names like Saddam Hussein, Tariq Aziz, Dick Cheney, acronyms like KTO and MOS—these became as well known as TV-commercial jingles.

This was a tough school, with tough kids, where threats of punishment were met with complete indifference. The kids did not normally pause to listen to anybody for anything. The Gulf situation was different. Let that TV in the upper corner of each room light up, let the principal say, "Please excuse this interruption of regular class time. I am going to give a brief update on the Gulf situation," and you could have heard a kid lighting a cigarette two bathrooms away.

People whose clothes were decorated with disgusting slogans had exchanged them for flag shirts and camo jackets and army-issue T-shirts. The school, which normally had a sluggish, hostile atmosphere, had a jubilance, an air of celebration.

A breathlessness.

Something was about to happen.

Not more class, not more tests, more trouble, more years.

But war.

There were eleven hundred kids in Wash: eight hundred were boys between the ages of fourteen and eighteen. Every single one thought war was swell.

Flag-raising, a duty that had been scorned for decades, was now a sought-after honor. Kids actually stood on the sidewalks—*not smoking*—as the flag was raised. Astle showed up one day with a cassette not of heavy metal or rap but of the U.S. Army Band playing the national anthem. As he turned it on and the flag went up, people came out of the building to stand at attention.

Desert Shield.

What a code name.

It spoke of soldiers over thousands of years, lifting their shields, protecting their shores.

Langan himself had never felt the slightest quiver of patriotism.

His mother was actually in the National Guard— the 333rd Quartermaster Petroleum, to be exact. Whenever the family went to see Mom's unit march, which it did for various Fourth of July or Memorial Day celebrations, Langan and his father would try not to laugh. Mom's Weekend Warriors were not very good marchers. There was always one person out of step, or chewing gum, or grinning at the crowds. Dad would mutter to Langan, "If this unit has to defend our shores, we're in deep trouble."

Rosalys Herrick had a shape as romantic as her name—spelled Rosalys, pronounced Rose Alice. Langan's mother taught kindergarten, and you could tell. She was sweet, bouncy, huggy-kissy, and petite. She seemed to have nothing to do with the uniform that wrapped her and the rifle that banged against her. A girl who had joined the Guard to pay her college tuition. A kindergarten teacher playing dress-up.

But an emotion Langan had never felt before now filled his heart. It was patriotism. He had thought patriotism was an act, like voting or knowing who was president during the Civil War.

Wrong.

It was a strange, heart-tearing energy. Like having a crush on a girl, but more intense.

Every morning, standing outside the school, watching the flag slowly move up the rope toward the shining ball on top of the pole, Langan's insides shivered. Maybe there was something wrong with him. Should you feel this way just hearing the word *America*? Should the sight of that red, white, and blue make you want to whoop and dance and march?

One day he actually felt a glaze of tears on his eyes and was desperately fearful that somebody like Astle would see.

But nobody did and he breathed easier.

The best thing about the Persian Gulf situation was that it gave everybody something to talk about. Something safe; something that would not make a guy belt you for eyeing his girl, or smash you for being racist, or trip you to get your lunch money for his cigarettes.

Everybody cared.

The black kids, the Italian kids, the Cambodian kids, the city kids, and the gangs.

In history, Mr. Grekula let them discuss one aspect of the Gulf situation for ten minutes every class period. He'd give a topic and anybody who got off the topic wasn't allowed to contribute for the rest of the week. Langan was absolutely amazed that after one mistake on one kid's part, nobody got off the topic again. They focused on the assignment as if they were about to be subjected to nuclear-biological-chemical warfare themselves.

- Is this fight over oil?
- Should the United States be the world's warrior?
- How bad is Saddam Hussein?
- What's the difference between this and Vietnam?
- What would you do if you were President Bush? General Colin Powell? Secretary of Defense Dick Cheney? General Norman Schwartzkopf?

Mr. Grekula was no fool. He put the ten minutes at the end of each class, and everybody knew they wouldn't get called on for opinions if they didn't behave for the first forty minutes. Nobody at Wash had ever learned so much in history.

By November, Mr. Grekula had talked the class (with the exception of two girls studying hairdressing and one guy who appeared to be brain-free) into reading the newspaper every morning in the study hall that preceded history. Two of the guys couldn't read, so Astle got permission from the hall proctor to read articles aloud to them. One hundred kids (so difficult they were at Wash mostly because their regular high schools couldn't control them) sat still while Astle read about the American troops already in Saudi Arabia, the problems of sand, the differences between Moslem culture and our own, and the hospital ships being readied.

On November 16, Langan raised his hand.

Mr. Grekula—who was not exactly sweet stuff himself—regarded Langan for a while. "Kid," he said, with what Langan hoped was affection, "I can't stand your name."

Langan sat very still. The entire class would pound him after school.

"Gonna call you Al from now on." Mr. Grekula looked at the rest of the class. "This here's Al," said Mr. Grekula. "Got it?"

The class nodded.

Why didn't I think of that? thought Langan. Just change my name myself.

Al.

He liked it. Solid, short, masculine.

Experimentally he wrote *Al* on the cover of his history book.

Mr. Grekula saw him and gave him two detentions for defacing school property.

"Aw, come on, Mr. Grekula," said Astle, "give the guy a break. He's only had a decent name for ten seconds. So he wrote on the book cover. Al won't do it again, will ya, Al?" Astle smiled at Langan. He had a smile both threatening and pixielike. Langan couldn't quite smile back. But he did manage to relax his frozen features.

Mr. Grekula looked as if he too—for once—might relax.

But the classroom door opened.

The principal walked in. He stood in the door looking oddly nervous—something a principal of an inner-city high school never looked. Or he'd be dead.

The class looked back. There was silence.

The principal cleared his throat and looked at Langan. His eyes were soft and sad, and yet—admiring? Envious?

Something's happened, thought Langan. Somebody's dead. Or hurt.

He thought of his father, his mother, his sister

and brother. His throat tightened. His features froze up again. He tried to breathe normally and could not.

Their last name was Herrick.

Three hundred years ago an Englishman named Herrick wrote the kind of poetry that gives poetry a bad name: *Fair daffodils, we weep to see you haste away so soon* stuff. But to Laura Herrick, a name made of poetry was right for her mother. *I sing of brooks, of blossoms, birds and bowers*, wrote the poet, and that was Laura's mother. Laura's mother was endlessly happy, and made happy by small things, pretty things, domestic things.

Laura Mary Herrick wanted to be the one named Rosalys and be a living poem, but Laura was born with the knack of getting terrific grades. Whenever there were parent/teacher conferences, her mother and father could bask in the compliments teachers paid. Laura had become an academic grind kind of girl and could not seem to extricate herself.

Her brother Langan purely hated school and found September through June pretty grim. He wasn't crazy about July and August either though, because Langan could not sit around. Summer just annoyed him. And he was only fourteen: too old for day camp, too young for work. Consequently, he spent most of his school career raising hell and humiliating Laura, who had never misbehaved in her life.

Laura had been delighted when Langan decided to go to Washington Vocational High. It was embarrassing, because Wash was a dumping ground for losers, but it left Laura on her own. School was hers, uncluttered by rotten brothers.

As for Langan, he now had a schedule that alternated three weeks of academics with three weeks of shop. He came home enthralled by new loves: he would be an auto mechanic, he would be an electrician, he would go into computer-aided drafting, he would be a carpenter.

It was required, during first-year vocational school, to take one week each of every one of the dozen shops offered as concentrations. Nobody could get out of any of them. The girls eager to be hairstylists had to suffer though auto-body repair . . . but the boys eager to go into auto-body repair had to suffer through hairdressing.

Langan's week of hairdressing was swiftly approaching.

Laura could hardly wait.

It was Langan's plan to be seriously ill that week, or else come up with a seriously ill grandparent across the continent, requiring his presence.

It was Laura's plan to inform the entire world. "Want a styling?" she would say to the girl Langan had had a crush on in eighth grade. "Langan here is going to become a beautician."

It was November 16. Laura smiled to herself, thinking of the humiliation her brother was about to endure. Revenge was not simply sweet, it was noisy and public.

Laura's year was not exactly a banner one. She was getting straight A's and running the silly Exchange Club, but life was boring. Langan was the one having fun.

She had had two major goals for sophomore year: to be a cheerleader and to sing in the choir. She'd decided these activities would lift her out of her Scholar Mode and put her into the Fun Girl to Be with Mode.

She made JV cheerleading and it turned out to be a very sweaty business in which she kept getting sore throats instead of dates with football players. She had lived through soccer, and basketball was to begin the same day as Langan's hairdressing. At least basketball was inside. She wouldn't freeze to death, and if she slipped doing a routine, she wouldn't be covered with mud.

Laura also got into the select choir but was forced to sing alto next to Jan Strick, whom she hated, and who hated her back.

Then the choir director mixed up the sections, for a better blend. Suddenly a baritone was sitting between Jan and Laura. A baritone named Kenneth

Thompson. Laura fell in love with Kenneth. Kenneth was extremely wholesome. He had a nice smile for everybody, a kind word and a helping hand. Laura's crush included a strong desire to get to the bottom of all that niceness and find Kenneth's nasty side. Of course, he was an only child. He had never had a younger brother or sister to corrupt him. Perhaps he really and truly didn't have a nasty side.

Jan graciously helped the romance along. Laura actually believed Jan when she told her that Kenneth was very active in the Exchange Club and therefore Laura should join the club in order to be with Kenneth.

Not that she had the time to spare, what with studying and cheerleading. But she joined. Instantly she was named an officer in a club of forty-five people hoping to be the student who'd go to Paris next year at the club's expense. Laura couldn't go; only juniors could go. But within minutes of walking in the door, Laura found herself arranging car-wash fund-raisers and setting up discussions involving French-Arab feelings toward the Gulf situation.

For Laura Herrick, the Gulf situation was of no interest whatsoever.

Last August 3 the news had broken on television, describing the events of the previous day. A dictator named Saddam Hussein had "swept" through the tiny Persian Gulf emirate of Kuwait, annexing it for his own country, Iraq. Laura herself could not tell Iraq from Iran, and felt it very thoughtless of these two countries to have such similar names. She also felt that "swept" was a rather domestic word for 350 tanks.

Saddam Hussein looked like a thug. He had the kind of mustache that you'd draw if you wanted to deface a photograph. He had a bad complexion and a huge toothy smile that he flashed at inappropriate times. Such as when gassing to death hundreds of his own peasants.

Saddam Hussein said that anybody who tried to stop him from keeping Kuwait would end up in a graveyard. He said he had a million soldiers to accomplish that.

A million soldiers sounded like enough to Laura. She'd leave him alone.

President George Bush said that Saddam Hussein invading Kuwait was "naked aggression."

Nah, thought Laura, I bet they were dressed.

Twenty-four hours later, the rest of the world was busy condemning Saddam Hussein for grabbing innocent little countries. Laura, grabbing her not-so-innocent little brother Nicholas, who kept going into her room and taking things that didn't belong to him either, guessed that Saddam Hussein was probably just as worried about the world's condemnation as Nicholas was about Laura's condemnation. "Get lost, Laura," said Nicky, continuing to grub among her belongings.

By August 5, there was price gouging at gas stations and American hostages had been taken in Kuwait. Laura did not pay attention. She read her horoscope instead and was gratified to find that she had a remarkable sense of humor.

On August 6 she caught her first TV glimpse of General Colin Powell, the chairman of the Joint Chiefs of Staff. America's most important military man. "He's cute," Laura told her father.

"Generals are not cute," said her father irritably.

The secretary of defense came on television. "Dick Cheney's cute, too," said Laura.

"Laura, could we please judge on the basis of their intelligence and leadership?"

"I don't know if they have either of those," Laura pointed out. "But they are cute." Her father, a loyal ABC watcher, flipped over to Cable News Network, shocking his family. "Stay with Peter Jennings," said Laura.

"Why? Is he cute, too?"

"Very," said Laura. Then she opened the newspaper herself, not with any thought of reading news, but to see what sales were going on at the mall.

By August 10 America was thinking of sending a huge military force to Saudi Arabia. Saudi Arabia was an immense stretch of sand south of Kuwait that Saddam Hussein also wanted to own. Laura, seeing films of the place, could not imagine why. Nevertheless, 250,000 American troops might be sent to Saudi Arabia to defend it.

Laura found that rather annoying. Why couldn't Saudi Arabia's own army defend it? It turned out they did not have their own army, which Laura considered rather foolish of them; what had they been doing all this time?

It turned out they had been pumping oil.

Laura had never heard so much about oil in her life.

Television made it sound as if America were going to go down the tubes in half an hour unless Saddam Hussein got wiped off the map.

Laura and her best friend, Kerry, were quite glad that school was about to begin. "Enough of this oil stuff," Kerry said. "Let's get back to basics."

"Boys," agreed Laura.

It was November 16, and Laura had a boy to worry about. Kenneth. He was immensely more important than Iraq.

However, Kenneth turned out not to be in the Exchange Club.

Jan had laughed for weeks.

Kenneth asked Jan out.

Laura sat in choir, singing next to a boy who made her heart turn over, arranging speakers for a club she hated, getting A's in classes that did not interest her, and when she went home she could not even watch any decent TV. Whoever got home before her was bound to have the news on.

The only news Laura Herrick wanted to hear was that Kenneth loved her instead of Jan.

Nicholas had always been the warrior in the family.

While Langan never cared for toy soldiers, never collected plastic dolls with miniature plastic weaponry, never constructed a fort from Legos or wore a miniature gunbelt, Nicholas was a war-toy kind of guy.

Langan loved tools. He scorned toy hatchets and plastic saws. From toddlerhood Langan took his father's real screwdrivers and real hammers and dismantled everything in sight. He went through a stage at age four of removing door-hinge pins.

Nicholas at age four had medieval knights with a castle and horses; he had cowboys with corrals and outlaws; he had cop cars and policemen who shot down drug dealers on dark streets under the kitchen table; and most of all he had GI Joes, armloads of GI Joes, and from the Legos, he built bunkers and tanks.

Nicholas still sucked his thumb. He would marshal his armies and set up his tanks. Saddam Hussein got the knights, cops, and cowboys, and America got the GI Joes. Then Nicholas would suck his thumb for a minute, pacifying himself, but not his war zone. Next, hanging his thumb out to dry, he'd play war, talking softly to himself except for when he shrieked POW! and ZAP!

Nicholas loved CNN.

He paid closer attention than any of them. At his age Laura and Langan had been learning the names of dinosaurs, but Nicholas knew the names of the planes and tanks being shipped into Saudi Arabia for the coming conflict with Iraq. If Laura glanced at the screen and saw a plane and said, "It's a Stealth." Her baby brother would correct her patiently, "No, Laura, it's an F one-eleven."

He'd sit in front of the television enthralled, his little mouth hanging open, his war figures half-positioned, as he watched the same news broadcast over and over again. Once he said softly to General Powell, "I love you."

Laura was in English and they were doing extemporaneous essays. Laura hated anything extemporaneous. She liked to have a week to do anything, so she could polish and perfect her work. This nonsense of having ten minutes made her ill.

She felt ill now. She did not always get an A when there was not time to think and revise.

She told herself that grades didn't matter, but for Laura that was not true. Grades mattered.

What was worse, the teacher had not given them a specific topic for the essay. "Write about what is bothering you most at this very moment," said the teacher. "Is it global? Is it family? Is it school? Is it friendships?"

Well, of course, Kenneth was bothering her most, and then Jan, but Laura was hardly going to put that down on paper.

The rest of the class smiled and started writing at the word "global."

Everybody but Laura was honestly involved in the whole Persian Gulf mess. Especially her family. Ugh.

Her father was fascinated by Desert Shield. He had so many problems at work that the problems of the world relaxed him. Tag Herrick was manager of the smallest branch of a small Connecticut bank, and Connecticut banks in 1990 were failing left and right. If they weren't failing, they were letting employees go and closing unprofitable branches. Her father did not know from day to day whether there would be a branch to manage, let alone whether they would keep him on as manager. He said he was well named: Tag—that was what he was playing, every day, just trying to stay in the game. If I'm fired, he would say at dinner, we'll be out on the street, penniless, carless, just a step away from homelessness. Laura and Langan paid no attention to this kind of talk. It was the father's job to have a job. It was the teenagers' job to go to school or fight with each other.

Dad found Desert Shield rather soothing: a bigger and far more interesting problem than his.

As for their mother, Rosalys Herrick had joined the Guard after Langan was born in order to get college-tuition money. Her unit specialized in pumping gas. She spent one weekend a month and two weeks each summer learning how to do this. It made Laura laugh. It made them all laugh. But they stopped laughing in late August when President Bush said he would call up the Guard to fight in the coming conflict.

The Herricks had been cooking out that night. Laura and Langan had spent the day down the road at Ellen's pool, even though Langan hated Ellen, and played some tennis, and then mowed the lawn (Langan) and worked on tans (Laura).

Laura was eating her potato salad slowly. She loved potato salad. She could have had this same menu every night all summer. "What does it mean—the president is calling up the Guard and the reserves?" said Laura.

Her mother was sitting very still. This was strange. Mom could not sit through a meal. She was always jumping up and down, wiping Nicky's mouth or getting more ketchup.

"Calling to what? I don't get it," said Laura.

"Usually," said their mother, "the active army goes to war. Then, to man the empty bases, the president fills in with reserves." She was not eating.

Mom—who felt that a hamburger off a charcoal grill was a good enough reason just to be alive.

"But this isn't usual?" said Laura.

Her mother wasn't looking at anybody either. Impossible. Mom was always grabbing their cheeks and kissing their lips or noses or foreheads.

Her mother said, "I telephoned my commander."

Langan and Laura laughed. They couldn't help it. A kindergarten teacher. With an army commander.

The face Mom turned on them was so severe Langan's laugh dried on his lips. "We might go," she said.

We.

We meant the family: Mom, Dad, Laura, Langan, and Nicholas.

This "we" was different. She meant her unit.

"Go where?" said Laura.

"Saudi Arabia."

"Don't be ridiculous," said Laura.

"I'm a soldier," said her mother. "My unit is trained to handle the fueling of vehicles used in war. Tanks. Self-propelled artillery. Jeeps. Trucks."

"*War?*" repeated Laura. "But you're my mother. Mothers can't go to war."

Her mother said quietly, "I am a soldier. I signed up, my country needs me, I'm well trained, and if my president calls my unit, I go."

During September and October, Laura left the room if discussion of war and mothers came up.

She would not have it. A mother going to war. It was sick and twisted and it was her mother.

Mothers had jobs at home: and her mother did them perfectly. Kindergarten teaching was a half-time job, so Mom could keep house, play with Nicky, bake brownies, and drive Langan and Laura wherever they needed to go. She might be a Weekend Warrior, but it didn't interfere; it was just part of the rhythm of their lives. Who did President Bush think he was?

But Laura kept that sentence to herself.

Everybody she knew thought that President Bush was pretty wonderful. He was going to show that bully Saddam a thing or two. America had the best air power and the most advanced equipment on the face of the earth, and Saddam Hussein was going to be sorry.

Or was he?

Saddam Hussein was not kidding when he said American soldiers would wade through their own blood. Saddam Hussein was not exaggerating when he said he would stack columns of American bodies and send them home to their weeping mothers.

. . . The door to Laura's English class opened. She disciplined herself not to look up. She was running out of time to write this silly essay. I will write on the topic *Not with My Mom*, thought Laura.

"Laura," said the teacher.

She looked up. The principal stood there. The

principal was a friend of her mother's; they took Jazzercise together. Mrs. Aymand said, "Laura, honey." Then she took a very deep shuddery breath and let it out like a puff filling an air mattress.

Somebody's hurt, thought Laura. Or dead. It's Nicky.

The little brother who tortured her life seemed incredibly beautiful and beloved. *No. He's all right. It isn't serious. He's going to be okay. He—*

"It's your mother, Laura," said Mrs. Aymand.

Laura could not breathe.

"She's been called up," said Mrs. Aymand. "Your father is coming to get you. You barely have time to say good-bye to her."

For a minute Langan could not even move.

His mother had been called up?

"They're going to the Gulf," said Mr. Ortiz. The principal was so excited he could hardly contain himself. "I'm going to drive you home. I guess you just barely have enough time to say good-bye."

Langan's lips did not move easily. "She—she's going straight to Saudi Arabia?"

"No. To her regular base. But she has to report this evening. I guess she's been on alert for some time, hasn't she?"

She had, but Langan had not really thought about it. This was his mother, not a soldier.

Langan was not getting up from his desk. He was having a hard time thinking what to do next.

Astle said. "Your mom is a soldier, Al? She's going to fight for America?" His voice was reverent.

Langan found his feet, found his books, found his tongue. "Yeah. She's in the Quartermaster Petroleum. Be pumping fuel into tanks and planes. Stuff like that. Front lines, probably. She always qualifies with her rifle. Every year."

The class was awestruck.

The tough black kids twice his size, the gangs of Italian kids whose jokes he didn't get—they were staring at him with envy and admiration.

"And don't call me Al," said Langan, swerving slowly to face every eye in the class. "My name is Langan. And don't forget it."

CHAPTER TWO

"What will you do when you get there?" said Laura. She was so nervous her teeth were chattering and she was grinding down to stop them.

"Same thing as always, I guess," said Mommy. "Smoke 'n' Joke." She ran the words into a slogan.

"But you don't smoke," said Laura. Laura felt horribly childlike, as if without Mommy she would not even be able to tie her shoes. She would be back at the age of scary things under the bed that only Mommy's voice could dismiss. Mommies couldn't just leave. Not when they had three children.

"Smoke 'n' Joke just means talking," said Mommy in what Laura always thought of privately as her hot-chocolate voice, as comforting as a cuddle. "Warming up. Getting yourself psyched to turn into a soldier for the weekend. Then it's: *a-tennnn-SHHUN!*"

The sudden, sharp-from-the-gut shout startled Langan and Laura so much they all but came to attention themselves. It made their mother giggle. "So then we get into formation," she said, "and the platoon sergeant takes roll call, salutes the first sergeant, and says, 'All present or accounted for.'" Rosalys had a slightly off-center smile, as if one side of her face were not as amused as the other. Laura had never noticed this before. What else haven't I noticed? she thought. She fastened her eyes on her mother, trying to soak up the face, the voice, the smile, and keep it like a pillow to cry into later. When the real Mommy was gone.

The uniform was baggy. Beneath it Laura knew Mommy wore bikini underpants and a violet bra with lace trim. What is she doing in that uniform? Laura wondered. What are we doing in this car?

Nicholas liked to play dress-up in his mother's army clothes, just as Langan had before him. When anybody spent the night, that person was sure to beg for the honor of clumping around the house in the heavy treaded boots, patting the empty grenade pockets. Everybody loved to wear Alice (All Personal Equipment Carrying Pack) over their shoulders instead of a dull book bag. And of course the

Kevlar helmet that fell over your eyebrows and squished your skull was best of all. There were buttonholes in the helmet's camo fabric for poking twigs into. Not that there would be much call for forest disguises in the Saudi deserts.

Laura did not want to be the first to cry.

Did Mommy feel like she was playing dress-up, or like a soldier going to war? Why were they chatting so normally, as if they were going to an amusement park and a picnic? Rosalys believed firmly in keeping your spirits up, and clearly she intended that nobody's spirits should fall even now, when the whole world was falling. Laura's heart rocketed in her chest like a loose missile and she was the first to cry after all. Langan kicked her.

"Then what?" said Langan quickly, so Mom wouldn't notice Laura getting all teary and dumb. Langan hated tears. One of the good things about vocational school was that nobody there expected you to be "sensitive," which was the big word back at the regular high school; "Be sensitive, boys, it's all right to cry," the guidance counselor liked to say, which tempted Langan to throw up instead.

"First sergeant calls at ease." Mommy said it the way her sergeant would: *HAT-ease!*

"Who's your first sergeant?" said Langan.

"Valerie Gutierrez."

He was used to Mom being a specialist. But a woman in *charge*? When they were going to *war*?

26

Langan, confused by the idea of a first sergeant named Valerie, looked away.

"Then she gives us the agenda for the day." Mommy smiled. "I expect this'll be a different agenda from the usual."

The usual. Weekend warrioring had been so "usual" that nobody even noticed. One weekend a month, Mom spent Saturday and Sunday elsewhere.

For Tag Herrick, who loved weekends, Saturday meant sports and Sunday meant movies. The family was equally willing to watch or to participate. In each season came Little League, then car races, ice skating, swimming. They had tickets to the Whalers' ice hockey games, they went into New York to see the Yankees (Nicholas always wanted to go to the zoo instead; their father, a long-suffering Yankees fan, said bitterly there was no difference). Sundays they went to a matinee. Mom and Dad did not mind even the longest drive to find a movie everybody could see. (They couldn't take Nicholas if the movie was too gory or sexy.)

When Mom had National Guard, weekends didn't change, except that Dad was more likely to do something dangerous because Mom wasn't there to stop them. Mom could be a real stopper of fun things.

As for summer, when Mom was gone two weeks, they camped on the beach at Hammonasset. How could you think about a missing mother when there was swimming and wading and teasing of lifeguards to do?

A missing mother.

Laura's eighth-grade history teacher had been convinced that soldiers Missing in Action from Vietnam were still alive somewhere in the jungles of Southeast Asia. Her ninth-grade history teacher, contrarily, said it was all piffle. Anybody labeled "missing" was bones under the mud by now.

Bones under the sand for this war, she thought. *My mother.*

Laura had no Kleenex. She used her sleeve.

Mommy's light-gold hair was tucked up under her camo cap. A few strands had come loose. What would the Arabs do to Mommy if they caught her? Would they hurt her? Torture her? Rape her? "Are you nervous, Mommy?" said Laura.

Langan looked at her, picking up on the "mommy." He said nothing.

"Of course I'm nervous," said their mother. "I'm sane, aren't I? But mostly I'm worried because I'm not in great shape. Years ago, after basic, I was in terrific shape. But I'll have to work awfully hard to get back. I'm saggy and soggy. I hate to think how few sit-ups I can manage." Mommy regarded her arms and thighs with disgust. Not with what Laura thought of as female disgust: bathing suits not fitting. Professional disgust: she had let herself go and might not do her job as well.

"Are you going to use a gun, Mommy?" said Nicholas.

"It's called a weapon," said their mother. "Yes, I am."

"No, you're not!" said Laura, horrified. "Women don't go on the front lines. They've said that on television a million times."

"I'm an infantry soldier," said her mother. "All soldiers learn all common weapons. Being a woman does not make any difference in today's army. I can use my M-16, the rocket launcher, the grenade launcher, and the M-60, which is a heavy machine gun."

Laura thought of enemy soldiers using the same weapons against Mom.

"I can also drive anything. You have to be able to drive whatever's there. The only truck I can't manage is the deuce and a half—it's a manual five speed so hard to shift even some of the bigger men have trouble with it."

"But you won't be on the front," said Laura. "So what difference does it make?" She pictured war like a diorama of toy soldiers at Revolutionary War battlefields: the farmers who would shoot for freedom behind trees at the river's edge, while the British in their red coats stood in exposed rows on the other side.

"Weapons shoot pretty far now," said their mother. "Miles and miles. Everything will be a front. It's not going to be neat, Laura. It's going to be very messy when it comes." Rosalys turned to face Laura. Her mother was determined not to tremble or fall apart. Laura could read that in her mother's lifted chin and quick-blinking eyes. "I can't tell you not to worry, sweetie," said Rosalys softly, "because there's so much to worry about. If I have to go—if it comes to that—"

"It's not going to come," said their father quickly. He patted his wife's knee. "Saddam Hussein is going to see what's arrayed against him and give it up. He'll pull out of Kuwait and say he's sorry."

"Oh, right," said Langan skeptically. "Dad, the man calls himself the Sword of the Arabs. He's bought thousands of tanks from Russia and China, hundreds of surface-to-surface missiles, hundreds of howitzers. He's the world's biggest buyer of chemical, biological, and nuclear weaponry. He wants to 'scorch' Israel. He just finished eight years of war on one border and he's lusting for more on another border. *Give up*? Come on, Dad."

"I was trying to comfort your sister and your little brother," said Dad stiffly. "What kind of help are you?"

"I think we have to be realistic here," said Langan importantly. "There's going to be a major, major, major war, with hundreds of thousands of casualties."

Langan was not the only one who watched a

lot of television news. "And blood," said Nicholas, nodding. "And land mines, and bullets and bombs."

"And hurt people!" shouted Laura. "Why do you guys talk as if this is something really, really neat? Those bombs land on people!"

"Iraqis, though," said Langan.

"Iraqis are people!" shouted Laura.

"I think," said their mother gently, "that there is much more chance of peace than war. I also think Mr. Hussein is going to be stunned by what's lined up against him. All he will need is a face-saving way out, and every ambassador on earth is trying to give it to him."

Langan looked disappointed.

Laura felt like hitting him. Maybe I should go into analysis, thought Laura. Other people think about sex most of the time. I think about hitting my brother.

How carefully Dad was driving the station wagon.

They were going exactly fifty-five. Of course everybody else on Interstate 95 was going seventy and it was purely dangerous to stick to the speed limit. Normally Dad would not have dreamed of keeping to the speed limit.

He doesn't want to get there, thought Laura. What does it feel like to carry your wife to war? Daddy was always first with the Weekend Warrior jokes. Now he's going to stay home and do the laundry and scramble the eggs, while his wife uses the heavy machine gun and drives the Jeeps.

Dad had a Jeep. He'd yearned all his life for a Jeep and had finally been able to afford it two years ago. It was his most beloved possession. Sometimes he went into the garage just to pat it.

Some weekends when Mom was warrioring, Dad would strap the kids in, grin his teenage grin, and press against the roll bar with his hand, testing its strength for the ride to come. Then they'd barrel at whiplash speeds up in the woods, lunging over rocks, skirting stumps, gunning through swamps. Langan and Laura and Nicholas would scream with delicious fear and come home perhaps with a bruised kneecap or a bitten tongue. They loved every minute of it. Who needed to go to an amusement park and pay for a fake ride when you could sit with your father and whack the top of your skull when he misjudged how far down the ledge lay? They loved thrill rides. One of the first things Nicky said clearly—clear to his family, at least—was, "Daddy. Wanna srill ride!"

Laura was crying anyway. Her eyes had begun without her permission.

In spite of her father's care, they seemed to be going as fast as attack jets, rushing down 95 at seven hundred miles an hour. Rushing to the end of life as they knew it. They were going to drop Mommy off, kiss her good-bye, and go home to a house without a mother.

She could not imagine this house.

Nobody home during the long afternoons. Nobody baking or neatening. Nobody making lists or kissing good night.

What would they do without Mommy? What would Mommy do without them?

Nicky, supposedly immobilized in his heavy-duty car seat, had managed to unzip Mommy's duffel and was taking everything out. Mommy had only the duffel and her backpack. Laura took more than that along just to spend a night at Kerry's. And this was all Mommy was allowed to take to her base: two packs.

Maybe that was good news, though. Maybe they would just train and train in Connecticut and never actually get flown to Saudi Arabia. After all, they had been called up, but they hadn't been assigned. There was a big difference.

Nicky had chucked the tiny, square *Book of Psalms* on the car floor. He had dropped the cassette on top: a recording from two Christmases ago when all the family had come to their house; every grandparent and cousin spoke on that tape. Since then, Dad's parents had died, so the voice collection was extra special. It would be Mommy's memory of home.

For some reason Laura never got quite as angry

with Nicky as she did with Langan. She hauled the duffel out of his reach, repacked it, and let him go on playing with the leather case of family photographs he'd gotten: a wonderful candid of Dad laughing in the driver's seat of the Jeep; Nicky swinging a tennis racket taller than he was; Laura sitting on a swing, pretending to be a femme fatale. In his photo, Langan was wearing his Bart Simpson T-shirt.

Mom leaned over the seat to look at the photographs too. "You know when we bought that T-shirt?" she said. "The same day in August that the United Nations set an embargo on Iraq. I remember because two of our aircraft carriers, the USS *Independence* and the *Eisenhower*, were within striking distance of Iraq, and I was thinking how inappropriate Bart Simpson T-shirts were for the occasion." Mom laughed. "You know what else happened the same day? Crayola Crayons retired my favorite color. Raw Umber." She joked with them. "I mean—guys. Crayon loss matters when you teach kindergarten. I saved my last Raw Umber crayon in the chest."

The huge sea chest in the upstairs hall where she put stuff like Nicky's first printing, Langan's first—and only—test graded 100, and Laura's French trophy.

Laura thought with sudden overwhelming horror that they had no souvenirs of Mommy in that chest:

nothing to remember Mommy by. No quizzes, no artwork, no printing. If Mommy died, what would they have left?

Laura's head swelled like a balloon, becoming huge and airy, and her thoughts spun dizzily.

Mommy frowned her list-making frown and studied her watch as if it contained as much truth as the Bible.

Or the Koran, thought Laura, thinking of the enemy's truths. Laura's terror faded slightly. The list-making frown was so familiar. A few months ago, she thought, Iraq was just some old country we bought oil from. Now it's a million armed men and a leader who wants Americans to wade through blood to reach him.

"Now," said Mommy in her line-up-for-the-story voice. "Let's think ahead. Be sure that everything is provided for. School's set. I arranged for my substitute in September when we went on alert."

"Stay alert," said Nicholas on cue. He had learned his first joke. He didn't understand it, but big people laughed when he said it, so he added, "The world needs more lerts."

Langan moaned. "Nicky, a joke is only funny the first time, and you've said that ten thousand times. Give it up."

Their mother ticked off problems, nodding to herself. "My curriculum is prepared through the end of the year. My sub has worked with me. She's used to my little girl in the wheelchair and the one whose mouth I'd like to sew shut. The class likes her. I don't have to worry about my class. Next. Fund-raising."

Rosalys was always chairing some committee. This year she was trying to raise one hundred thousand dollars to replace the church's steeple, clock, and tolling bell. Dinner dances, trips to ice-hockey games and the opera, pledge campaigns. . . . "John Leigh was my vice-chairman for the steeple," she said, exclusively to her husband. "Poor soul. Figured it was safe because I like fund-raising." She shrugged, writing off the energy poured into the steeple effort. "He raises it or he doesn't. Now. We changed the bank accounts. I'll be earning about the same thing on full-time army as I do half-time teaching, so income's not a problem. Next. My will is written."

"*Your will is written?*" said Langan.

"You have to have an up-to-date will," said his mother briefly.

"What's a will?" said Nicky.

"Shut up," said Langan to his brother.

I'll inherit the last Raw Umber crayon, thought Laura. I'll bury my mother. All that will be left is stuff. Junk. Things. Laura began to sob out loud.

"Shut up," said Langan to his sister.

"You, Langan," said their mother, "will never say that again. I am counting on you to be a help. You are the older brother. You will take care of your younger brother, pitch in, and do your best. And that's that. Clear?"

Langan hated being told how to behave.

"Answer me!" she said sharply.

"It's clear, Mom," he said reluctantly. But it's not fair, he thought. She gets the good stuff. She gets the war and the uniform and going overseas and a unit and tents. I'd give anything to have that! And she's sticking me with her dumb four-year-old. That isn't fair!

"But what *is* a will?" persisted Nicholas.

Laura had never seen a corpse. What would a dead woman look like?

But this was not actually a ride to death. Not yet. It was more like a trip to divorce. Here was their exit. Here was the red light. Here was the road that led to the Armory. In a few minutes they would be separated from Mommy, with walls and barbed wire and even weapons between them.

Laura studied her father's reflection in his rear-view mirror. He was about one breath away from sobbing with her. Dad: whose idea of emotion was to offer everybody a second wedge of pizza.

Laura felt out of breath and thin. Her tears dried up as if she were on a desert herself.

"A will," said Mommy, "is a piece of a paper that says what to do next if something goes wrong."

"Oh, good," said Nicky. "Daddy has a list, then?"

Their mother was big on lists. Especially for errands and groceries. She wrote the lists in pencil and crossed things out in ink.

"Daddy has a list," agreed their mother. "Now. Rides. Daddy isn't home until six-fifteen every night. That means after-school activities are a problem because I won't be around to chauffeur. Langan. Your swim meets. You'll have to get a parent to drive you both ways. That's your responsibility, Daddy can't get to it. Laura, your piano lessons and JV games. You've got to arrange that. I didn't have time. You each have dentist appointments coming up. Hope and Johanna's mother will probably help. Don't be shy about asking for rides or else you won't get anyplace."

Laura hated to ask for rides. It made her feel weak and helpless. She especially hated riding with Hope and Johanna's mother, who was brittle and sarcastic.

Rosalys went on listing. "Now. Nicholas."

"Yo!" shouted Nicholas, who had learned this syllable from Langan and used it constantly.

Mommy's voice turned falsely bright, teacher-style. It was a tone of voice Laura particularly detested, and yet somehow she loved her mother even more as Rosalys shoveled on the cheer. "You're already in morning day care, sweetie, and you know how much you love the Pumpkin Patch! Now you'll stay afternoons too! Won't that be neat? You get to take naps and have outdoor play and afternoon arts and crafts just like the rest of the boys and girls! Isn't that nice!"

"No," said Nicholas.

"Have I left anything out?" said their mother.

They were in New Haven.

At the Armory.

The place was not a madhouse, as Laura had expected, with the ninety members of the unit due within the hour. But it was different. There was not going to be any cruising in, looking around, waving at people you recognized. A guard stopped them where they had never been stopped before.

It's military, thought Laura. Before, they were Weekend Warriors, and they knew it. Now it's real, and they know it. *I don't want it to be real!*

Mommy got out. Laura got out. Daddy hefted the backpack and duffel, and set them on the pavement. Langan freed Nicky and the boys scrambled out.

Mommy ran her hands over Langan's face, tracing his features. She knelt beside Nicholas and hugged him, her eyes closed, her chin trembling.

Three more cars arrived, depositing three more members of the 333rd. Two black men and a Hispanic woman tugged at their uniforms, said goodbye to their families, and looked across at the empty sky and the ugly city with blind eyes.

Mommy said briefly, "Hey, Jarall. Luz. David."

"Hey, Rosie."

Rosie? Her family looked at her. Nobody, but no-body, called their mother Rosie. She loved her full name: Rosalys.

"They call you Rosie?" said Langan.

Mommy smiled. The smile was tight and fake. "Only out here. We get inside, I'm Herrick."

Laura started to sob uncontrollably. She tried to smother it, bite it back, chew on it, but it welled up out of her and became huge and noisy. She was ashamed and desperate.

But her mother hugged her as only a mother can hug. "You be my good girl. I love you," whispered Mommy. Inside the hug, Laura was two inches taller. She could not bear it. This tiny woman going to war? How could a country send its wives and mothers to fight? "Mommy, don't go," she whimpered.

Even Nicky wasn't whimpering. He was too awe-struck by the size of Jarall's boots.

Mommy had saved Dad for last, like dessert. Their hug was a bear and a half. Dad's eyes were wet and his hands were shaking, but he said noth-ing. Perhaps he couldn't. Or perhaps everything had been said already, in the privacy of their marriage, where Laura had never been and could never see and never hear.

Mommy stepped back. Straightened her uniform. Smiled at Jarall, Luz, and David, who were waiting for her. Each army face was both strong and yet falling apart from emotion. Their complexions were so different, their sizes so different, but their faces matched. Fear and love, in equal parts.

"Mommy, don't go," whispered Laura.

"I have to go, baby," said Laura's mother. "Even though I'm your mommy, I'm a soldier. I'll always be your mommy, never forget that. I'll be back as soon as I can. But right now I'm in the army and my President needs me."

CHAPTER THREE

They were celebrities.

The neighbors brought casseroles, as if Mommy had died.

Dad had no idea what to do with the food. He stood with the Corning Ware dish in his hand mumbling, "Um. Noodles. Right."

Nicholas said, "Is it stuck?" He lifted the aluminum foil and sure enough, the foods were stuck together. Nicky would not touch food that was stuck to other food. You put mushrooms and sauce and pimientos and chopped ham in with the noodles and Nicky felt it was nothing but heated-up vomit.

Laura gushed, "Oh, thank you so much! This will be so yummy!"

"No, it won't," said Nicky. Laura hauled Nicky into the kitchen. "Shut up," she hissed. "You can have a hot dog."

Nicky said he was sick of hot dogs. He wanted pizza. He wanted Mommy. When was Mommy coming home?

"Not for a while," said Laura. Her patience, never extensive, began to wilt. She stuck a Popsicle in Nicky's fist and called it a day for nutrition.

"Come look at the news!" screamed Langan.

Laura raced into the TV room, whacking her elbow agonizingly against the wall.

Channel Eight in New Haven was showing Mommy's unit. The blond reporter, whom Laura disliked even more than the *other* blond Channel Eight reporter, was doing the interviewing. "You may be going to war shortly," said the reporter, moving her lips as if she had just gotten braces. "A war against a nation reputedly armed to the teeth! Better prepared and far more practiced than any army the world has ever seen! Are you afraid?"

The camera panned over men in camo suits, cheerful as kids going out on Halloween. The reporter poked the mike in the face of a black man who grinned. "Sure I'm scared, but we're ready. We've been doing this a long time. We know what we're doing. I'm pretty eager to show what we can do." He was young and sweet looking, with Afro hair cut in spiral designs.

Laura studied him carefully. Wish they'd show Mom, she thought. How come they're only showing men? There are eleven women in the unit.

The microphone moved to another face, so handsome she wanted him to be a movie star. He was black too, but a lot darker than the first one. He grinned, down-home and sassy. "Anybody says he's not scared is lying," said this soldier. "All we talk about is how scared we are. Nobody wants to die. I'd rather die than lose my legs or my eyes, though. That movie where the guy is paralyzed after Vietnam? Forget it. I'm not doing that. No way."

Laura had thought of death, but not mutilation. Mommy might come home with one leg? With no eyes?

The next man was white, and old. Older than anybody. He looked fifty. "Do they let people that old in the army?" said Laura doubtfully.

"He was already in," explained Langan. "Probably been in for decades."

The blond reporter blinked her diamond-bright eyes. "Many members of the National Guard never thought they would go to war. They joined for college tuition or for extra income. Many Guard members are shocked and angry that they have been called up. Do you feel the president had any right to do this to you?"

The older man raised his eyebrows. "We're surprised, but I don't know anybody who's angry. As for whether the president has a right, of course he has a right. That's the point. He's president. We're his army."

The reporter was disappointed, as if she had hoped to find a soldier trying to back out. That would be deserting, thought Laura. I don't want Mommy to desert, but I don't want her to go. Maybe I could kidnap her.

Langan liked what he was seeing. The men looked solid and sturdy and decent. Even the youngest one sounded like he knew what he was doing. Langan was so envious! They were going to see things and do things and he was going to be stuck in school. There would probably never be a war for him. These guys would wrap it up in a week.

Though lots of people were afraid it would be like Vietnam, and last for years, and kill hundreds of thousands.

Langan had heard that they were getting ten thousand hospital beds ready to treat the wounded. Ten thousand! Like ten of his high school, every single person shot and bleeding.

Except me, thought Langan. I wouldn't get hit. I'd know what I was doing.

The second black man took the mike back, an experience the reporter was not used to. Her eyes followed the missing mike instead of the soldier. "We're proud of who we are," said the young man.

"We know what we're doing, we do it well, we all believe President Bush is right, and we're Connecticut Yankees going out there to do a good job.

"Awwwww-right!" said Langan enviously. He hoped Astle was watching. And Shawnee.

"Speak for yourself, man," said a soldier off-camera. "I'm from Rhode Island."

The soldiers laughed, slapping each other's backs, and the picture returned to the desk in New Haven where the anchor people simpered, as if war was amusing, a parlor trick conjured up to fill news time.

"Were those Mom's friends?" said Nicholas.

"They'd better be," said their father.

Which was when the phone rang, and they remembered that they had forgotten a very important phone call.

"It's gotta be Grandma and Grandpa," said their father. He closed his eyes. He did not get along with his in-laws. Their annual visits were too long for Dad even if they stayed at the motel. "You answer it, Laura," said her father, and she knew, absolutely, that she had just inherited all the unpleasant chores.

"Hi, Grandma," she cried cheerily. Langan rolled his eyes. Dad headed for the door. "Don't let Daddy out," hissed Laura, and Langan agreeably tried to get his dad in a headlock.

"It has been several hours since you took your

mother to her unit," said Grandma sharply. "We have been sitting by this phone all night long waiting for details."

Mom had had so much to do that she hadn't managed to dial Grandma and Grandpa Forsey until the car was packed and ready to head for New Haven. The good-bye had been brief, with Grandma and Grandpa crying, "No! No! No!" and Mom saying, "I'll be fine, don't worry, Tag will call the moment he gets back."

The moment had stretched into about eight hours.

"I'm sorry, Grandma," said Laura, feeling sick and rude and unkind. "It's been hectic. Mommy hardly even knew she was going and then she was going, and now she's gone."

"Hey, brilliant sentence," said Langan. "Maybe the president would hire you as a speech writer, Laura."

The cord didn't stretch far enough for Laura to kick her brother.

"Of course I'm proud of my daughter," said Grandma, sobbing, "But I never thought it would happen. I never, never believed I would live to see the day my darling little girl would fight like some common soldier. Of course if your father had earned enough to pay for her college degree, this would never have happened."

"Mom is a common soldier," Laura pointed out.

"And she seemed very proud of it when we left her at the Armory."

"Did you take pictures?" demanded Grandma.

"No, but you must have seen it on TV."

"Laura, please use your head," said Grandma. "We are hundreds of miles away. Our TV station is certainly not going to broadcast what is happening in the city of New Haven, Connecticut."

Laura kept her temper. "Would you like to speak to Nicky?" she offered.

Their grandparents loved the baby of the family far more than the difficult teenagers. Laura, who could remember being adored, and Langan, who could not, resented it.

Nicky grabbed the phone. He was still thrilled by a phone call. What do I mean, still? thought Laura. If Kenneth called me up right now to see how we're doing, I'd be pretty thrilled.

She was proud of how diplomatic she had been with Grandma. She turned around for her share of praise to find Dad and Langan hadn't noticed. It was only Mommy who spotted things like that and told you how wonderful you were.

"Do you miss Mommy, Nicky?" cooed Grandma, her voice loud enough to reach Saudi Arabia. "Mommy's gone far, far, far away, Nicky. For a long, long, long, long time."

Nicky was stunned. "Far?" he said anxiously. "Long?"

"Do you want Grandma to come and stay instead?"

Dad whipped the phone out of Nicky's hands before Grandma could do any more damage. "Thanks for the offer to come down," he said, "but we're doing fine. You know your daughter. Rosalys arranged everything perfectly."

At last Grandma and Grandpa were off the phone. "I bet they call every night," said Langan.

"I bet they do too," said Dad gloomily. "Come on, Nicky-nicks. Bed."

"Not till I say good night to Mommy." Nicholas stood firm in his blue cotton pajamas, legs spread, hands on hips.

"Mommy's gone."

"Go get her," ordered Nicky.

"She's in the army now. The president has work for her to do," said Dad.

Nicky narrowed his yes suspiciously. It sounded pretty unlikely to him. "Then let's call her up," said Nicky.

"We can't, kiddo. They wouldn't let Mommy have a phone call."

"Is she in prison?" said Nicky worriedly.

"No."

"There were guards. And barbed wire."

"It's where her army is," said Daddy. "Come on. Bed."

It was a nice idea, but nothing short of police restraints would have kept Nicky in his own bed. He circled the house, getting in bed with each of them in turn, socking them in the stomach when they refused to produce Mommy, and moving on to the next bed.

"How long is a long, long, long time?" he kept asking. "Grandma says it'll be a long, long, long time? How long is that? How long?"

"We don't know!" they kept yelling.

Nicky would not accept that. They were big. They had answers. They were just being mean.

At one o'clock in the morning, Laura grubbed in Mommy's closet until she found an old, dark green army T-shirt. "Here," said Laura, figuring either this worked or she'd just kill Nicky now and end it all, "this is the very same shirt Mommy is wearing right now for work. It even smells of Mommy." Laura dumped some of Mommy's perfume on it. Then she pulled off Nicky's pajama top and replaced it with the T-shirt, which reached his toes. "I want dog tags, too," said Nicky.

Daddy and Langan were of course faking sleep. Mommy had not been gone overnight and already Laura was handling all the hard stuff. And she was so tired and strung out she wanted to throw Nicky down the stairs. "Mommy had to wear the dog tags herself," Laura said, "but you can wear her pearls." Mom had started wearing pearls when the president's wife did. Rosalys loved Barbara Bush. Laura got the biggest strand and put it around Nicky's neck.

Nicky patted his pearls.

"Where do you want to sleep?" asked Laura.

"With Langan."

Laura hoped Nicky would wet the bed. On purpose, she didn't take Nicky to the bathroom first.

Langan really was asleep, not faking. His mouth was half open, his half-grown body sprawled over the bed like Superman about to fly. Nicholas tucked himself into the curve of his big brother's arm and fell asleep.

In his army T-shirt and pearls.

Washington was a school of factions and gangs, of people who carefully steered around each other or calculatedly started trouble with each other. Langan had just become the only kid in the entire ninth grade who could instantly join any group and be welcome. *His* mother was going to fight for America. *His* mother was part of Desert Shield.

It was a heady experience. Langan swaggered a little, joining the Italian gang that used knives and then going over to the Cambodian gang that used invisible fishing wire. But mostly he sat with Astle and with Shawnee, the only two kids with whom he shared every class. Shawnee had the largest boobs in America. Langan could not figure out how she balanced herself. Langan felt honored and weird to be a trio with Astle and Shawnee.

It surprised him that he was thinking much more about new and growing friendships than about his mother maybe going to the Gulf. It seemed pretty unreal. Especially for Rosalys Herrick. Whereas having a friend or two, after three months of tiptoeing around trying not to offend anybody, was very real and very desirable.

Mr. Grekula was talking about earning money. Mr. Grekula liked this subject much more than history. Yesterday he had discussed laundromats and how you could make a fortune owning one. Today it was snow throwers, and how in a good winter, lots of snow, you could make a fortune owning one.

Langan definitely wanted a fortune. Other people could have allowances or piddly little minimum-wage jobs. He had not been interested in the laundromat fortune, but he liked the snow-thrower fortune.

Langan visualized himself with a fortune. It was a nice picture.

You could buy a snow thrower at Sears, said Mr. Grekula, for eight hundred dollars. Sign up thirty driveways at twenty-five dollars apiece, that's seven hundred fifty dollars in one snow. Six good snows, you're making over thirty-five hundred bucks even after you've paid for the snow thrower? Huh? Whaddaya think?

Langan thought how worried his father was about money, his job at the bank, and Connecticut's economy. Langan would buy a snow thrower and be raking in the dough all winter long.

He told Astle and Shawnee about his master plan. Astle was very impressed. Shawnee was not. "What if it don't snow?" said Shawnee.

" 'Course it'll snow. This is winter." Langan was thrilled. He could hardly wait to get home and study the Sears catalog.

"This is Connecticut," Shawnee pointed out, "where winter's a wimp."

Langan ignored that.

"How you gonna find eight hundred dollars anyway?" said Shawnee.

She might be big and black, but she sounded exactly like Langan's mother.

"I'm gonna charge it on their Sears card," said Langan with dignity.

"They're gonna love that," said Shawnee. "You need a place to live after that, we got an extra cot."

Astle grinned at Shawnee and changed the subject. "How's your mother?" said Astle.

"We haven't heard from her yet." Langan wouldn't tell his mother about the snow thrower until he was rich. In fact, maybe the best thing to do would be to get the mail each day before Dad got home and discard the Sears bill. Plenty of time to earn snow money before the second notice came.

* * *

Laura could hardly wait for chorus.

Assuming she managed to arrive.

Passing periods were like wedding processionals: she walked very slowly so as to be able to smile and say hello to everybody who said hello to her. The whole school knew that Laura's mother had been called up. Laura's mother was the only soldier they had, and they wanted a big photo of Rosalys to hang in the lobby.

Flags were everywhere: red, white, and blue from birthday-cake miniature to stadium size. Flags had sprouted overnight on hall walls, bulletin boards, hairpins, and T-shirts.

Their neighbor had rushed over that morning with a rhinestone American-flag pin for Laura to fasten to her white sweater. It caught everybody's eye. All the girls wanted one.

In chorus, the music teacher said she was changing some of the music they had planned for the Christmas concert. "We're going to substitute *The Navy Hymn*," she said. "It's a prayer, really, for servicemen and women at sea and on the land and in the air."

Everybody looked at Laura.

Laura felt like Princess Diana. She tried to be lovely and shy at the same time, to accept the homage and not overdo it. She almost waved and bowed but stopped herself in time.

Kenneth said to her, "Is it going okay at home?"

"Pretty good."

"It hasn't even been twenty-four hours," said Jan waspishly. "I would think even Laura could manage so far."

Mistake, thought Laura, rejoicing.

Kenneth glared at Jan. Then he turned his back on Jan and said to Laura, "My mother wants to write to your mother. She says the troops need mail every day. And chocolate-chip cookies."

"Mail and chocolate-chip cookies?" repeated Jan, laughing. "The woman is a soldier, Kenneth. She's some tough broad who—"

"Shut up, Janet," said the music teacher with a ferocity that gave Laura a queer shiver. But when she thought about it, Jan wasn't so far off. "It's okay," said Laura calmly. After all, what Rosalys *needed* to be was a tough broad. "My mother *is* a soldier. And she *is* tough."

The class about swooned with respect.

Laura had to yank her stomach muscles in to keep from laughing with delight.

Celebrity was pretty decent.

They had been watching a lot of news since August 2. They had kept up to date on hostages, reservists, and the billion dollars a month—or was it a week?—or a day?—that this was going to cost the United States. They found out that soldiers in the desert had to drink four liters of water a day to combat the hundred-and-twelve-degree heat. They knew that Saddam Hussein said if America and her allies so much as looked his way, he would turn them into "columns of bodies." This would be, he said, the Mother of All Battles. Saddam did not mean your loving gentle mother, he meant some brutal mother who slaughtered her own children.

Since Mommy had been called up, television news had became a member of the family.

They watched continually, mostly ABC or CNN, hungering for details that might apply to Mommy and tell them whether Mommy would actually go to the nightmare location on the Persian Gulf.

The television-ness of their new world was complete. The Herricks had always loved television. But this was not a situation comedy, a rerun, an old movie, a forbidden talk show, or a quiz. This was—or it was supposed to be—a war.

To Laura, it remained a stage set. Producers had rented a desert somewhere and lots of tanks. They had old films of aircraft carriers and stern generals. Their artists drew terrific graphics.

Often Laura saw nothing on the screen she didn't see during *Jeopardy* or *Little House on the Prairie*. A display case. If she climbed into the television set, she'd be surrounded by klieg lights, cameras, and a studio audience. Saddam Hussein would peel off his mustache. Even when real-life individual soldiers were interviewed, it was little more to Laura than laundry-detergent ads, where people are amazed at how white their whites get. Laura was amazed at the concept that any of this was really happening. That it included her mother, and even Laura.

Then suddenly she would believe it all too grotesquely, complete with blood and gore and burials and orphans, and she would have to go to her room to sob. When the sobbing stopped, she would go back downstairs, where the TV would still be on, still playing the war show.

Laura began losing track of where her mother was. Sometimes Rosalys seemed to be next door in New Haven, giggling like Laura over being called a tough broad. Other times she seemed thousands of miles away, hung with weapons, dodging missiles, striding through the sand.

"The United States," said the network, "is threatening an all-out, decisive, multifront assault on Iraq."

"Sounds like war all right!" said Langan, wildly excited. The entire nation was coming together, like a great big vocational high school—saluting flags, and not smoking, and getting misty for soldiers in uniform. Langan was thrilled to be living in a television generation. He would get to watch the Mother of All Battles as It Happened.

Dynamite.

The television commentator was stern. "And how

will this affect us . . . on the domestic front? Home values . . . are down. Inflation . . . is up. Joblessness . . . is up. Banks . . . are failing."

Herricks, thought Laura, in the same rhythm, are losing their minds.

"We are going into," said the commentator, "a recession. And now—"

His voice hung threateningly.

"And now," said the commentator, "*war is just a trigger away.*"

Langan whooped a wild and wicked war cry, picked up his little brother and used him for a submachine gun. "Ah-ah-ah-ah-ah-ah-ah!" shouted Langan, killing the wall. He and Nicky laughed joyfully.

Langan dropped Nicky onto the sofa, where he bounced.

"Shoot me again," said Nicky, holding his arms up.

CHAPTER FOUR

Laura could not look at movies in which there were great heights. Any movie that showed a cliff, or skydiving, or hang gliding, left Laura's palms icy and her heart pounding. Heights gave her the sick feeling that she had no floor to her, that she was going to fall out the bottom of her world.

But in movies, you could close your eyes: blot out the Grand Canyon or the hot-air balloon. Then the floor came back into your feet and heart and mind.

Not now.

Not with this.

Mommy being gone was bad enough, but Mommy intensively training to get ready for war

. . . there was a hole in Laura's strength. She was losing herself. The anxiety did not go away. She never seemed to have enough breath in her lungs or enough sleep at night.

Laura had never liked being alone in the house at night. Eyes stared from the black outdoors. Evil sifted under the windowsills. Murder crawled up the cellar stairs. Laura liked every light on and every door locked, plus a friend on the phone if by some horrible chance she found herself alone after dark.

Now, no matter who was home with her, Laura remained alone in the dark. The house was invaded by Laura's fear.

And the television . . .

She could not bear to have it on. All that talk. All those experts. All those retired generals and admirals. Their emotionless unmoving mannequin faces. Lips that hardly moved discussing the chances of death and destruction.

The television had no subject except war.

Nothing mattered but Desert Shield, the generals, the soldiers, the president . . . and Saddam Hussein.

But she could not bear to have the television off, either. Because if she turned it off, something might happen. War might begin. Peace might be arranged. Bombs might drop. The 333rd might be ordered to Saudi Arabia.

(They were calling the country Saudi now, because Saudi Arabia took too long to say. Except Langan: he was calling it Sau.)

Mommy was not even in Connecticut anymore; the 333rd had gone to Massachusetts for more intensive training.

The house was full of Laura's anxiety. There was not one shred of Mommy's calm control. The family did not settle into a routine. Her father was used to sharing tasks. He had never made up the lists of what to do, or decided when to do it. And in spite of Mommy's master lists, taped to the refrigerator, there was not enough time in the day to do any of it.

They lasted eight days, which was roughly the amount of groceries, laundry, and good humor they had.

At this point, the entire house fell apart. Nobody had clean underwear. There was no milk. There was no loose change for lunch money. None of the pens wrote, so Dad couldn't sign the permission slips. The car was out of gas.

On the ninth morning, at breakfast, Langan stapled his book report together and tossed the stapler onto the kitchen-desk shelf. He missed, and the stapler dropped right into the bacon grease still hot in the skillet.

Nicholas decided that he was never going to eat cold cereal again in his life, and made the point clear by dumping his Cheerios on the table and blowing them across the room.

Laura got both bacon grease and Cheerios milk on her shirt and smacked both her brothers.

Their father came running downstairs from his shower, freshly shaven, well dressed, eager to grab a piece of toast and run with Nicholas, only to slide on the milky floor, skid into the stove, and get bacon grease on his suit.

Langan had no clean jeans, in spite of the fact that he distinctly remembered one more pair on his shelf. While his father was swearing about the suit, Langan saw that his worthless rotten crumby jerk sister Laura was wearing his jeans. He began ripping them off her legs. "Dad! Make her wear her own clothes!" screamed Langan.

"I didn't have any clean jeans either!" screamed Laura. "And he has more jeans than I do anyway, it isn't fair to start with. Dad! He's trying to hurt me. Kill him!"

"Look, Daddy," said Nicholas. Nicholas was still in his T-shirt and pearls, which he had worn every night since Mommy left. "They're gonna both be dead."

"Good," said their father. "It's simpler that way." He ran upstairs, changed clothes, and stuffed the grease-laden suit in a plastic bag to drop off at the dry cleaners. He ran back downstairs and realized that his four-year-old was not dressed. Screaming wordless howls of frustration, he raced to Nicky's bedroom, grabbed clothes, popped them in a paper grocery bag, scooped Nicky under his arm, and headed for the side door.

"The day care is going to be furious if you make them dress Nicky one more time, Daddy," said Laura. "You'd better dress him first."

"And take those pearls off him!" yelled Langan.

"If I am late to the bank one more time, I'm on their hit list!" shouted their father. "On top of everything else, you want a father who's unemployed? You want to be on welfare? You want to eat oatmeal for the rest of your life?"

Nobody in the Herrick household would have eaten oatmeal for a split second, let alone a lifetime.

"Take off the jeans," said Langan to his sister, "or die." He flourished the Swiss Army knife with its seventeen sharp attachments.

Laura was not entirely sure he was kidding. She gave him the jeans.

Their father was back in the house. He was purple in the face, eyes bulging as if somebody from one of the Cambodian gangs at Wash, with the invisible fishing wire, were strangling him from behind. *"What is in the garage?"* he screamed. *"Langan Herrick! What is—"*

"It's a snow thrower, Dad," said Langan. "Don't worry about it. I know what I'm doing. Go to work."

"*Whose is it?*"

"Mine, Dad. Keep your shirt on."

Their father threw Nicky across the room into Laura's arms. Nicky almost swallowed his pearls. Dad grabbed Langan by the sleeves. "*Where did you get it?*"

"Sears."

"*What? What are you talking about? Those things cost hundreds of dollars! What are you doing, selling drugs?*"

"Dad," said Langan, really getting annoyed.

"How did you pay for it?"

"I charged it."

"*You? Charged? It?*"

Langan tasted death. His father was very close to the edge. Langan, whose specialty was being wise, wiseassy, or downright snotty, said very softly, "I'm going to earn thirty-five hundred dollars this winter, Dad. It'll pay for itself right away."

"You have a charge card yourself, perhaps?" said his father.

Langan's school bus honked out front. "I can't miss my bus, Dad," said Langan quickly. "It's fifteen miles to school. You've gotta drive Nicky. Laura, grab the pearls. Bye, Dad. No problem, huh? Don't worry, we'll be rich, Mr. Grekula says so."

His father bellowed out the door, "When I come home you'd better have called Sears and gotten that goddamn thing returned or you are dead meat, you little turkey!"

Television, thought Laura. This is television. We are being paid to act like this. Nobody's family on earth would act like this except for money. Mommy's in a television war and we're in a television comedy.

Laura stared at her brother and her father. For several moments they really did seem like actors to her, doing a fine job on a stupid script. Only a very stupid writer would come up with a little boy wearing pearls and a T-shirt anyway. It wasn't their *life*; it was their *act*.

Even their front yard was some grotesque parody of real front yard.

A woman at Dad's bank had given him twenty yards of yellow satin ribbon, which Laura thought was the queerest thing she had ever heard. Dad said during a war you tied yellow ribbons around your trees. No: *that* was the queerest thing she had ever heard. Sure enough, Dad had tied a bow around each of the three big maples in the yard, like apron sashes.

There was nothing Laura hated more than people laughing at her.

Laura went to school wearing a skirt she particularly hated. She felt fat and ugly in it. She was mad at her father for not planning better and her brothers for being alive. She would have been mad at her mother as the source of all this trouble, but it seemed unpatriotic to blame Rosalys.

One good thing: the entire town had picked up the yellow ribbon mode. Ribbons flew in the wind, sagging around little branches and whipping off car antennas. Ribbons decorated picket fences and storefronts and hung on front doors like Christmas wreaths.

"How's life?" said Astle.

Langan shook his head. "My dad has a real attitude problem."

"Toward you or Saddam Hussein?" asked Shawnee.

"Right now," said Langan, "I'm not sure he knows the difference."

"Told you so," said Shawnee happily. "You go use his charge card for some dumbo machine ain't gonna work anyway cause ain't gonna be no snow, you gonna have serious problems at home, buddy."

Langan hated the way girls always said *told you so*.

The school newspaper was doing an article on "Our Troops and the Gulf War." Laura, being the only student with her own personal troop, was of course the major interview.

She loved it.

Four of the top, top kids in school, each with a

notebook, one with a camera, one with a cassette recorder, seriously and anxiously asked her questions already drawn up and okayed by the top English teacher.

Two of these top, top kids were top, top boys. Laura wondered if they would be smitten with her, and ask her out, and love her forever, and it would all be due to President Bush. Or even Saddam Hussein.

"Is it difficult adjusting to your mother's absence?" asked one of the top, top girls.

Laura almost said, "It's horrible and we hate it," but caught herself. The key here was family togetherness. Paper over those cracks. "Oh, no," she said, letting amusement surface. "We had quite a while to prepare, you know. We couldn't let my mother down by doing any less than our best." Laura almost gagged at the sound of that prissy garbage, but the four interviewers wrote it down in quotes and sighed happily, like Langan hearing a fighter pilot promise to kick butt.

"Do you hear from your mother much?"

"She telephones every few days," said Laura. All her brothers wanted to know was whether Mommy was using a gas mask yet. On TV everybody talked about gas masks, which would have to be worn because Saddam Hussein would be dropping chemical bombs on the troops. Mommy said she was excellent with her gas mask; eight seconds to put it on, plenty of time after warning was given.

"We sleep in an airplane hangar!" her mother had said. Laura could not understand how her mother could sound so pleased and energized. The last thing her mother should be doing was enjoying herself.

"It is *frigid*, Laura! The hangar is open to the winter. Our cots line one end. There's no privacy. Along the walls are tables where the coffee urns, ham sandwiches, and candy bars are. We train till we drop and then we play volleyball. We are so excited! We're wired. I mostly hang out with Starr."

Starr was her best friend from the unit; they'd been together the whole decade that Mom had been active. Starr was a black social worker at the city hospital.

"Does your mother know if she'll actually go to Saudi Arabia?" said one of the boys, his eyes as jealous as Laura's.

We all want to be there, thought Laura. We don't want it to be happening, but if it is, we don't want to be left out. Everybody my age—we're left out. "If she does know," said Laura slowly, "she isn't telling us. Maybe it's classified."

But the unit would go. She knew, Dad knew, Mommy knew, the whole unit knew: it was just a matter of weeks. Or days. You could not wage a war without fuel; the 333rd was ready, its equipment was new and plentiful, its members trained . . .

Saudi Arabia. Sand. Missiles. Death. Mutilation. *Distance.* Mommy would be so very gone!

Laura started to cry. What kind of soldier am I? she thought. She tried to remember soldiers' words, and finally came up with some. Voice breaking, she croaked, "That's the president's choice and we'll find out when we find out."

The top kids were reverent. They waited for Laura to pull herself together. One of the boys actually handed Laura a handkerchief: a snowy white cotton rectangle. Unused and everything. All her life Laura had wanted to weep on a boy's shoulder and be comforted with his handkerchief. Except she had never met anybody before who didn't use Kleenex. She smiled at him. He smiled back.

"What exactly does your mother do?" said one of the girls.

Laura had been a little worried about this one. "The unit is responsible for fueling," she said. "They fuel ground vehicles: tanks, fighting vehicles, self-propelled artillery, Jeeps, trucks. And they're responsible for storing the fuel, and moving it along with the vehicles."

She did not know a single detail more. "Mom, go pump gas, will ya?" was the family joke. They had not been sufficiently interested to know things like what did the gas come out of, or into. What the dangers were. What the tools and tasks were.

Her mother must have chosen to keep her two lives separate.

One Saturday, years ago, Laura, usually asleep when her mother left for Guard duty, happened to be wandering around in her nightgown. Mom picked up her gear as casually as a laundry basket, jerked her garrison cap backward down over her hair, and trotted out the door. She had not seemed like a mother, but like some unknown soldier passing through. The way she walked, held her equipment, and tugged down the cap had not been Rosalys. It had been Specialist Herrick. Somebody Laura did not know.

"Did your family start talking about this right at the beginning?" asked one of the boys. "Did you begin planning in August?"

"My mother did," said Laura. "But she protected us from worrying about her." Waited till the last minute to let us be a part of the worry and the planning, thought Laura, feeling a sudden rage at her mother. Mommy left us out. Langan and I are fourteen and fifteen, and she treated us like Nicholas. As if we would just be in the way.

"Is your father proud of your mother?"

"Tremendously!" said Laura. "He's really, really proud of her."

Actually, Laura had no idea how her father felt

about Mommy. Sometimes Dad was as full of anger as a wasps' nest. And yet when he spoke of Rosalys, his voice was gentle. He had taken the dusty old wedding gown portrait from the upstairs hall and propped it beside the TV. CNN would show sand and desert and Arabs with their red dish-towel headgear, and smiling beside them would be sweet young Rosalys headed down the church aisle to Happily Ever After.

"Are you scared?" said the boy with the handkerchief.

Laura just looked at him. "Saddam Hussein says he's going to turn our columns of troops into rows of bodies. This is going to be the mother of all battles!" She hated that phrase of his. It turned "mother" into something ominous and threatening. "Of course I'm scared."

He gave her a sudden intense hug. "She'll be all right," he said huskily. "I'm sure of it, Laura."

The hug was wonderful. She didn't ever want it to end.

But of course it ended instantly, and instead of asking for her hand in marriage, the boy trotted off with the others talking newspapery things like column inches.

Still, it gave her courage.

Boy courage.

She went straight to find Kenneth, before she panicked.

She detoured into the girls' room first, to check her hair, teeth, lipstick, and clothes. She was in the stupid skirt but that couldn't be helped now.

This was the time.

She knew where Kenneth's locker was. Laura knew where all the terrific guys' lockers were. And he was there. Handsome, sweet, nice, wonderful Kenneth.

And he was alone.

Truly, thought Laura Herrick, God is on my side in this war! "Hi, Kenneth," she said. He can't really like Jan, thought Laura. Jan is such a rotten piece of work. A nice guy like Kenneth: he's only going out with her because he hasn't picked up the signals from me. I'm his type. I'm nice too. Whereas Jan—ugh. She'd as soon stab Kenneth as kiss him.

"Hey, Laura. How's it going?" Kenneth's smile made her knees weak. "You hear from your mom?"

"She called two days ago. I guess the training is pretty intense."

"I heard she's been practicing with gas masks."

"Yup. They have to be ready to face that madman." Laura leaned up against the lockers and looked into his face. Kenneth switched books and shut the door firmly.

"You don't lock?" said Laura.

He shook his head. "I never leave anything like a jacket and nobody seems to want my chem-lab book."

They smiled at each other.

Before she could panic, blubber, or perspire, Laura said swiftly, "Kenneth, would you go with me to the tenth-grade dance next week?"

Kenneth stared at her, confused and unprepared. He looked back at his locker for a moment and then down at his unlaced high tops. "Umm." Kenneth was trying to think of something kind to say. "Thanks for thinking of me," he said at last. "But I'm taking Jan. I mean, like, we're going together."

She wanted war to break out right then; a few bombs dropping would have interrupted the scene just fine, but of course nothing happened, and she had to walk down the hall with Kenneth anyway.

"I could—um—let's see," said Kenneth desperately. "Pete hasn't asked anybody. I'm friends with Pete. I could—uh—"

"It's okay," said Laura. "Never mind. Really."

At the school door, Kenneth fled.

The late bus left promptly, five minutes past the end of after-school activities. She had missed it. She walked across the parking lot. It was a long hike home. The November evening had already come, and it was raw and damp and ugly out.

Kenneth actually liked Jan. What was the matter with boys? What were their standards, anyway? Did they even have a standard?

She got a ride one block from school. Two boys from the basketball team who wanted only to talk about her mother, and Desert Shield, and did her mother have any inside information?

They aren't interested in me at all, Laura realized. If this were a month ago, they'd never even have noticed me by the side of the road. Even if I were unconscious and bleeding. It's my mother they notice.

Laura wanted to cry. She wanted her mother. She wanted to talk with Mommy and use up a box of Kleenex together and agree about how horrible men were.

"Thank you for the ride," she said stiffly. She dragged herself into the house.

The three men in her life were all home.

And they were all horrible.

Nicholas was sobbing and hauling on the belts of his brother and father to make them shut up.

Langan was shouting. "Listen to me! I know what I'm doing! Don't worry about it! This is a perfect investment!"

Dad was screaming, "Eight hundred dollars! For some stupid machine that'll break the first time, assuming there *is* a first time, because every other year it doesn't even *snow*!"

'I'm going to pay you back!"

"You're going to return the goddamn thing! Don't

you dare use my credit-card number without permission."

"I am not going to return it! I signed up twenty-two driveways and sidewalks for this winter, and that's what I'm doing!"

"You're going to do what you're told!"

"I told my customers I'd clear their driveways!"

"You don't have any customers, you little—"

Grandma and Grandpa Forsey telephoned at that moment, of course.

"Laura, darling," said Grandma. "How's everything going? Are you getting along? I know you won't be able to manage without your mother."

Laura hated it that Grandma could be right, especially about this.

"I'm not home," called Dad. The men in her life—just like Kenneth—fled, leaving Laura to make up lies about how well they were doing.

"Let me speak to your father," said Grandma.

"He's not home," said Laura.

"Not home? Suppertime on a school night? Where is he? Who is fixing the meal?"

"He's getting groceries," said Laura.

If only it were true. They were so completely out of groceries that the cupboards actually were bare. The only stuff left was the canned goods you gave to the church welfare bin because nobody at home would eat them.

He should have gotten groceries, thought Laura, furious with her father. I don't care about his dumb dry cleaners, or getting Nicky, or his stupid bank. He should have gone to the grocery first. I don't care how tired he is, either. I'm tireder. And I had a worse day. And how am I supposed to get groceries? Do I drive? Do I have a station wagon? Do I have money?

She was ready to slug him by the time she went into the TV room. Of course they were listening to an expert on the Middle East. Who were these people? What did they do when they weren't being experts? "Nobody in America," said the expert sternly, "understands Arabs." But clearly this was the kind of slipshod, careless upbringing he had come to expect from Americans. He launched into a crystal-clear (for retarded American minds) description of Allah, Moslems, and holy wars.

Laura hated him. She hated all men today. Where were the women experts when you needed them?

"Who is Allah anyway?" asked Nicholas.

"It's another name for God," said their father. "That's what Arabs call God."

"What do we call God?" said Nicholas.

"We call him God."

"Why don't we call him Allah?"

"Because we're Christian."

"Why?"

"Because our parents were."

"Why?"

"Because we're Anglo-Saxon. From countries that were Christian."

"Why?"

"Maybe we should have supper," said their father.

"Maybe we should go shopping first," said Laura.

"Maybe we should order pizza," said Langan.

"How many days has it been?" said their father.

"Nine."

"You realize she could be away six months," said their father. "We're gonna have to get our act together."

"Tonight?" said Laura, who was starving.

"Maybe over the weekend," said her father. He fell asleep in his chair and eventually Laura boiled spaghetti and they ate it bare: they had no sauce, no butter, and no cheese.

Laura had a sudden desire to call up her old friend Kathie Ferguson, long gone out of state. Poor old Kathie. In one single year, Kathie's mother divorced her father, remarried, divorced her new husband, and remarried Kathie's father. Meanwhile, Kathie's father had had a hair transplant and two affairs, one with a woman much older and one with a woman much younger.

Whenever Kathie tried to eat lunch in school, everybody would swarm around, demanding the latest episode in the Ferguson Family Soap Opera.

Laura remembered vividly how they had howled with laughter at each turn of events. How nobody had the slightest sympathy for Kathie at all, because deep down, nobody believed any of this stuff. Real parents didn't do that.

For the first time, Laura realized that Kathie must have suffered, wept, hurt, ached, been outraged, fought back—all those things. And not one of her high-school friends had given Kathie's sad and desperate year a thought: it was just a another television show for them.

I could call Kathie, thought Laura, if I knew what state she went to. Kathie is probably the only girl on earth who'd believe that my formerly acceptable family has no food in the house, no intention of shopping for any, is reduced to eating bare spaghetti, except for the mother, who is qualified to teach the alphabet but instead is going to fight Arabs.

If this were TV, thought Laura, I would turn it off.

And yet it *was* TV, and if she turned it off, she would not know what was going on. As for the bad show her family was putting on, Laura did not know how to turn that one off.

She couldn't swallow the pasta.

"Pretend it's war rations," said Langan.

Laura didn't want to pretend anything. She wanted her mother, she wanted Kenneth, she wanted not to have been humiliated, she wanted somebody to comfort her when she cried, and she wanted tomato sauce on her spaghetti.

CHAPTER FIVE

Thanksgiving vanished out from under them; they didn't have one. Mom had to stay at her base. Dad finally rallied and took the children to a restaurant where they glumly lined up along a buffet for slices of turkey somebody else had cooked and pumpkin pie somebody else had baked. How could you give thanks when your mother was gone?

It turned into December before you could catch it and stop it.

Christmas wreaths went up with the yellow ribbons, and lights glittered in stores. Trees were being sold in every parking lot and carols played in all the shops.

"I don't even know where our Christmas decorations are stored," said Laura. She didn't even know if she wanted to put them up without Mommy. Then it occurred to her that President Bush would never send the troops to Saudi Arabia at Christmastime. That would be un-American and also just plain mean. Sure, there were a few hundred thousand Americans there now, but they had gone overseas back in August and September, when Christmas was too distant to count.

We're safe till January, thought Laura.

Mom called pretty often.

"What do you guys do all day long, anyway?" said Langan.

"Practice," said Mom. "Get our equipment in order, practice some more, and then practice. Plus lectures."

"Lectures?" said Langan. This was terrible news. In the army you weren't supposed to be subjected to that kind of thing.

"Today's was on how different the culture of Saudi Arabia is. How we women especially must not be upset about the principles of the Saudis. Saudis are very strict with their women." Mom laughed. "Starr wants to know why the Saudis don't have to worry about *our* principles? Since we're doing the fighting for them."

"Good point," said Langan. "Why don't they?"

"Because," said Mom, "we are guests in their country."

"And what did Starr say to that?"

"She said she's been correcting people's attitudes for many years now and hates to stop when she has her speed up."

With every call, Mom went back to being kindergarten teacher; she rallied them, encouraged them, cheered them on. She even talked that way to Daddy, Laura could tell by Daddy's expression: he hated being comforted and he didn't like offering comfort either. He just wanted everybody comfortable automatically.

With Mommy gone, nothing was on automatic.

They had conquered groceries though. It turned out if you all went to the store on Saturday and bought every single thing in sight, you would have enough to last till the following Saturday. And Daddy had made up a list of his own, for meals. Meals were not going to be exciting. They were shoppable, though.

Monday, hot dogs. Tuesday, hamburgers. Wednesday, macaroni and cheese from a box. Thursday, pizza, delivered. Friday, spaghetti. Saturday, more hamburgers. Sunday, with any luck, thoughtful neighbors would have them over.

When it was her turn on the phone with Mommy, Laura never had anything to say. What was she supposed to do—whine about Jan? Whimper about Kenneth? Moan over the tenth-grade dance? Complain because she was doing laundry more often than Langan was? Tell on Langan about the snow thrower?

The snow thrower had not been returned.

Dad forgot about it during the day and every evening he and Langan had a ritual fight over it before Dad fell asleep in front of the news.

The weather was cold, but not very. Much too warm for snow. Langan listened even harder to the weather reports than to the war reports.

"School's pretty good," Laura told her mother, although school was pretty bad since she had humiliated herself with Kenneth. "Basketball season started. We have a good JV team. Cheerleading will be more fun than soccer was because in soccer we lost so many games. I hate cheering for losers."

Some people actually thought American soldiers could lose the desert war. That Saddam's Mother of All Battles would be American's globally public humiliation. How would the country cheer for losers? What would happen to America if deep down they weren't the best on earth, but were just plain old losers?

Oh, how Laura hated thinking about a war! "Mom?" she said, thinking of Thanksgiving and home and fireplaces, although they didn't have a fireplace. "Do you want me to send you stuff like your knitting projects? Or your quilt pieces?"

"Baby," said her mother softly, "I think you think

I'm still mommy here. Still a homemaker and a kindergarten teacher and a soprano."

But you are.

"I'm a soldier, Laura. This is real. This will be real bullets, real bombs, real chemicals, and real desert sun. The weapon I'm carrying is not a toy for Halloween."

"I don't want you to go, Mommy!"

"And I don't want you to worry," said her mother firmly. "I am confident there's going to be a peaceful solution. The secretary general of the United Nations, the president of France, the king of Jordan—they're all working on it, they're all talking to Saddam Hussein, they'll come up with a compromise."

No way José, thought Laura Herrick. We're talking two countries here that think compromise is wussy. Saddam Hussein would get his whole country plastered before he'd be a wuss. Same for George Bush.

Langan had stared at maps of the Middle East so often he knew the boundaries of Saudia Arabia, Iraq, Kuwait, and Israel better than Connecticut's. In what his sister referred to as "the olden days" (prior to August 2), Langan had had only the foggiest idea of where Saudia Arabia was, and he had certainly never heard of Kuwait. Back then he had said to his father, "Why do we care about this?"

"Oil."

"Why does Saudi Arabia care about this?"

"They're afraid Saddam Hussein will decide to conquer them next. Everybody's nervous when there's a bully in the yard."

"And the Saudis are our friends?"

His father had laughed. "If you count anybody in the Middle East as a friend. Friendships between the USA and Arab countries come and go. But right now, yes, they're friends, and they're threatened, and President Bush says we can't let our friends go down the tubes."

"Not to mention our oil," put in Langan.

But back then he had not cared enough. He was much more concerned that Nadav Henefeld, the six-foot-seven-inch basketball player for the University of Connecticut, was going to play the next season in Israel, his own country, instead of returning to U Conn. Langan and his father were very worried. What would Coach Calhoun do? Would they still be a winning team?

Now it seemed impossible to Langan that he had spent a molecule of brain power on basketball.

There was so much else to think about. Like Israel.

The Arab world hated Israel. The experts said that if Saddam Hussein could get Israel into the war, then no Arab country would fight against Saddam Hussein after all; it would be their bounden duty to line up against Israel. All Saddam Hussein had to do was drop a few bombs on Jerusalem, and the famed Israeli air force would be airborne within seconds, retaliating.

Then the picture would change!

Then the allies would shift!

Then the excitement and war would begin!

And then there was always money to consider. Langan loved thinking about how much money he was going to earn. He couldn't wait for snow. He saw himself outdoors, in the harsh white cold of winter, the engine of his snow thrower throbbing under his skillful hands, the ten-dollar bills collecting in his fat wallet.

He'd make thirty-five hundred this year, but with the profits he'd buy a used truck, a wood chipper, a chain saw, an industrial-strength lawn mower; next summer he'd probably make thirty-five thousand dollars, doing yard work for the people whose driveways he'd faithfully plowed.

"Did you go into the gas chamber yet?" Langan asked his mother when she phoned. Every soldier had to get ready for the moment when Saddam Hussein would unleash his horrendous chemical-gas power, trying to drown them in poisoned air. Soldiers rehearsed in a gas chamber, where they had to take off the mask and breathe in the gas! This was to give them faith in the competence of the mask. Langan presumed it was fake poison gas, not real poison gas. What if somebody screwed up? Now there's a lawsuit, thought Langan.

"I did that years ago, in basic," said his mother. "You never need to do that a second time, Langan."

Langan should be so lucky.

At least I have my snow thrower, he thought. I may not have a war, but I can make big bucks.

Grandma and Grandpa Forsey telephoned the same night. They were upsetting, which was normal. Grandma kept telling Dad that the way Mom "triumphed" over the "tremendous burden" of being a working parent was to make lists.

"Lists," said Grandma. "That's the key. Get your lists made, Tag, and stick to them."

"Thank you," Dad said woodenly.

"Stay calm, Dad," Langan advised softly.

"The person who charged eight hundred dollars of my money on some stupid machine that will never work is telling me to stay calm?" hissed his father.

"Dad, Dad," said Langan gently.

"I'm not your collie dog," said his father. "Don't tell me how to behave. The minute we're off this phone, we're calling Sears and getting that thing picked up."

Nicholas, however, stinker that he was, told. "No, nobody's getting along," said Nicky to his grandparents. "You should see Daddy and Langan fight. Wham! Bap! Kazoom!" He smiled joyfully into the phone. "Plus," he confided, "I get to wear pearls to bed."

It took some time for their father to tell enough fibs to satisfy the grandparents that all was well in spite of what Nicholas claimed, and by the time he got off the phone he had forgotten about Sears again.

They were just thinking of things like homework (Laura) and money (Langan) and ice cream (Nicholas) when the phone rang again and it was Mommy again.

"Hi, Mom," said Laura. "We just got off the phone with Grandma and Grandpa. Ugh. Nicky was rotten. And I forgot to ask you. Where are the Christmas decorations?"

"We're leaving, Laura," said her mother quietly. "It was just announced."

"Leaving what?" said Laura.

"The United States. Thursday we fly to Saudi Arabia."

CHAPTER SIX

A state-long parade.

Langan was extra glad about it being a Thursday—he was missing a history test; sometimes problems had gifts. As far as Langan was concerned, this was the adventure of all time. The families were going up in a parade to Westover AFB in Massachusetts, from which the 333rd would leave. Hundreds of vehicles—parents and friends and reporters and Vietnam vets, politicians and truck drivers who were just in the mood—formed a caravan, starting at the Armory in New Haven, and going up I-91 to Massachusetts.

Banners hung from overhead bridges: WE SUPPORT OUR TROOPS IN SAUDI ARABIA!

Homemade signs were taped to the rear windows of cars: GOD BLESS AMERICA!

SADDAM, YOU'RE TOAST, was Langan's favorite.

Local veterans' groups in each town mustered displays and marching bands. Free coffee was available at every truck stop.

Patriotism punctured Langan like buckshot. He was wild and exhilarated and screaming with delight. "Honk the horn, Dad!" he yelled, and his father leaned on the horn long and loud.

Langan held up his first finger for Number One, and then his thumb for Way to Go, and finally made the V sign for Victory.

He was the luckiest person in Connecticut. Everybody else had to go to school and take a test. He got to be part of the war.

FAREWELL! said some of the signs. FAREWELL AND GOOD LUCK!

It's a real word, thought Langan, who never thought about words.

Farewell.

Fare well.

Do Well. Stay Well. *And good-bye.*

While the three men in her family shouted and laughed and honked the horn, Laura used up her Kleenex supply.

Saddam Hussein—with his half million men, his

weapons, his vicious, evil fighting techniques, his poison gases, and his incendiary bombs—Saddam Hussein was taking their mother.

Although they were not a combat unit, every member of the company carried M-16 A-1 rifles. Rosalys wore her flak jacket and carried the chemical suit (wrapped up in itself to make a package), while her canteen and gas mask bumped against her sides. Her hair was invisible under the camo cap. Laura thought it gave her a streamlined, military look, to be without hair.

The trip from Westover AFB to Saudi Arabia would last thirty hours. Although the base was in Massachusetts, the company was from Connecticut, so the governor of Connecticut had come to see them off, bringing individual bakery cakes for every soldier. Each cake was iced in an American flag. Everybody was pleased to have a tasty snack for the plane, but nobody knew how to hold it, considering they each had eleven hundred other things to carry in only two hands.

One enterprising soldier—he looked about eighteen—solved this by setting his cake on a table, putting his face down into the icing, and scarfing it up.

My kind of guy, thought Laura.

She tried to burn their faces into her memory, thinking—these are my mother's buddies. That's the word they use in the army. Buddy. Not friend, not roommate, not fellow reservist. But buddy.

Such a little-kid word. A word for when you went swimming and weren't supposed to go in alone.

But that's what this is, thought Laura. They're going swimming, and the ocean is full of tanks and missiles and poison gas, and if they ever needed a buddy, it's now. She thought, *Take care of my mother, you buddies, you.* But her mother was older than most of them. Laura thought her kindergarten-teacher mother would be the one taking care of that cake-eater and probably half the unit. She wouldn't be home taking care of the family.

Mom scooped Nicky up, hugged Laura, and kissed Langan all at the same time. Langan, who normally would rather have cancer than be kissed, kissed her back.

Mom pointed out all her buddies. Jarral, Starr, Luz, David.

Nobody knew what to say, so they babbled, had some cake, and studied the governor and the crowds, and hoped the TV cameras would pick them up so they could watch themselves tonight.

In the rear of the hangar sat cargo helicopters. The only helicopters Laura had ever seen were the traffic guys for radio stations. These army helicopters were as big as a house.

Dad took Nicky and Langan over to inspect one

and left the girls alone. Laura and her mother hugged, the way mothers and daughters can hug but sons and fathers never can. Her mother's expression was intense and fiery, like an explosion.

"Mom?"

Mom squeezed Laura's hand hard and let out a breath of pent-up air. "Oh, Laura, *I'm so excited.* I cannot wait, Laura! I'm out of breath every second thinking—*I'm part of this! I'm going.*" Her mother hugged herself. She looked quickly toward the rest of the family, assuring herself they were not in hearing distance, and turned back to Laura as if they were best friends, talking girl to girl. "I love my life, Laura, don't misunderstand me. I love my family—especially you, the boys, and Dad—and I love family things, from making chocolate-chip cookies together to bowling, and I love teaching five-year-olds . . . but . . . that's my life. That's it. I've never complained because there's nothing to complain about. But Laura! I've never had an adventure before . . . I'm going to war. I'm going abroad!"

Rosalys, mother of three, was not thirty-eight at that moment: she was a teenager, pink-cheeked with pleasure.

She's going to have fun, thought Laura, and after her surprise she was both glad and jealous. "Does Dad know?" she said.

Her mother turned thirty-eight again. Sober and worried. "Your dad's never had an adventure either.

He . . . it's a lot to think about, Laura. His wife is going to war and he's staying home with the kids. His wife will shoot a machine gun and see a desert and fight an enemy and he'll do laundry. He's not envious, because he's afraid for me, he's afraid about the whole thing. But he's—"

"He's envious," said Laura.

"Men go to war," said her mother.

"Not now," said Laura. "Not this war."

There was a pause. Carefully, as if English were her second language, Rosalys said, "We have to talk about the possibility that I might die."

"No!"

"I know it will be hard on you," said Mom, her eyes twinkling and her laugh spurting out the sides of her mouth, "but I've decided that Nicky gets the pearls."

Laura laughed through her tears.

"You're the toughest one in the bunch, sweetie," whispered her mother. "Don't let me down. Your daddy and your brothers don't have your spine. Be my strong girl."

They held all four hands. Laura felt her mother's bones. She wanted to talk on and on, to share the adult thoughts, the marital history, the subject of men versus women (surely the most interesting subject of all time). She wanted her mother to tell her why a nice person like Kenneth would prefer a stinker like Jan, and she wanted her mother to say that Kenneth would wake up one morning soon and be sorry he had lost Laura.

But Dad, Langan, and Nicholas were back, and the moment was over, and Rosalys turned into another person altogether. A strangely stiff woman, looking over a horizon to a place none of her family had ever looked. Then she handed each child an envelope. "I wrote letters," she said slowly. "Do not read them now. It's for if I don't come back. It's what I have to say to you if you have to lead your lives without me."

She was not looking over the horizon to Saudi Arabia.

She was looking at her own death.

Fear assaulted Laura like fists. She could not look at anybody, she was not sure she even had eyes to see anymore: she was as enveloped in fear as if Saddam Hussein had bombed her with it.

"I wanna see you put your gas mask on," said Nicky.

"Sure," said Mom, relieved to have something to do. "Want to time me? I'm terrific." She was, too. Finished with a second and a half to spare. She became a monster, with jutting parts and tubes. Her voice was deformed by the mask.

Nicholas began to cry. "Mommy!" he wailed.

"What's it like in there?" said Langan.

Rosalys pulled the mask back down so it rested under her chin like a second head. Nicholas kept crying. "Tight quarters," said their mother. "The first time I was afraid of the mask. But we do it so often now I'm used to it." She tucked her dog tags into her shirt. The shirt pockets were embroidered: HERRICK on one and U.S. ARMY on the other.

If she gets killed, thought Laura, that's how they'll identify her. Pieces of metal and embroidery. That's what they'll send home of her. That's when I'll read the letter. When the officer comes to the door.

The ceremony began.

The ninety soldiers stood apart in neat rows, while the governor mounted a podium and the families huddled together, stranded in the vast hangar.

The governor was very tall, very large, very authoritative. He said, "I have been informed that the president of the United States has exercised his authority pursuant to Section 673B of Title 10 of the United States Code and ordered a unit of the Connecticut Army National Guard to federal active duty for a period of one hundred and eighty days. This action has been taken in support of the current United States operation in the Middle East."

Laura had not known there would be a ceremony.

She had not known her heart would stir and her skin prickle and her eyes glisten when those flags were raised, those uniforms lined up, and those speeches began.

All the spectators had flags in their hands.

Nicholas was looking around and learning. He was like that at day care: very observant, very eager to pick up any cue. He held his flag in his right hand, waving it just like everybody else.

"Don't drop your flag, Nicky," whispered Langan.

Nicky looked at his brother as if he were road kill. "Think I'm stupid?" said Nicky. "I don't drop flags."

"Sssshh," said Laura.

General Gereski spoke next. He said, "I have full confidence in the men and women of the 333rd. They have trained continuously for the possibility of hostility. I am sure they will represent the state of Connecticut and this country well."

A very small girl next to them, high on her mother's shoulder, suddenly crowed with delight. "Hi, Daddy!" she called.

"Shhhh," whispered her mother.

"Hi, Daddy!" the little girl shouted.

Nicholas opened his mouth.

Langan muttered, "You yell hi to Mommy and I'm putting you through a wood chipper, Nicky."

Nicholas thought better of saying hi to Mommy. Instead he transferred his flag to his left hand and carefully studied how people were holding their thumbs up. It took him awhile to get his hand turned around so his thumb was up for victory. "Is this right, Langan?" he whispered.

It was the thumb that Nicholas sucked. It was withered and wrinkled like dead tissue.

"There's going to be a silver lining," Laura murmured to her father. "Nicky's thumb is going to dry out."

Langan thought his mother looked very professional. He was envious of the whole outfit. The camo, the rifle, the gas mask.

She's not looking at us, thought Langan. She's forgotten us. She's really listening to the general's speech. She wants to know what he has to say. She might actually die there, or lose an arm or her eyesight or her best friend, and she wants to know what she's doing it for.

Laura held her father's hand. He gripped hers tightly. His cheeks were wet with tears. "Rosalys," he murmured.

Across the hangar, Rosalys straightened, as if she had heard his panicky whisper. She took a quick sharp step to the side, falling into a new line with her unit. She saluted, and held the salute, staring firmly ahead without moving a muscle in her face, looking—

—military.

The woman was a soldier.

Indistinguishable from all the rest.

A defender of America.

Langan, who had been all energy, wilted. Joy and

patriotism had exhausted him. He was so proud of her.

A large blaring voice, like the voice of God, came from speakers around the immense hangar. "Soldiers of the 333rd Quartermaster Petroleum Company, you have five minutes remaining with your families."

Five minutes.

Laura's eyes filled with tears and her heart with panic. Mommy, don't die, she prayed, don't die, don't die, don't die.

Five minutes! thought Langan. Mom is so lucky. I wish I could go instead of her. I hate being fourteen. I hate being a kid. I hope the war lasts. I want to go, too.

Nicholas said, "I have to go to the bathroom."

They left Westover AFB and began driving south, back to Connecticut, back to home.

Nicholas was not a good car traveler.

Let's face it, thought Langan, Nicky isn't good at much of anything.

Usually they bribed Nicky to stay quietly in his car seat by throwing food at him. They had forgotten to bring food.

"I remembered everybody's coat," said Dad. "I remembered the good-bye presents to Mom. I remembered the camera and I remembered a second roll of film. I remembered to fill the gas tank. But do I get credit for anything?" asked Dad. "No. Nicky just wants more."

"I wanna stop for a treat," wailed Nicholas.

"No!" yelled Langan.

"Why not?" yelled Nicky.

"Nicholas," said Laura, "we can't have a treat when Mom is going off to Saudia Arabia. It's not fair. This isn't a party. We don't get ice cream."

"Why not?" said Nicholas. "We had cake at the base. And it's a long way home."

"Shut up," said Langan.

"Han-go-burs then," said Nicholas, who had never gotten this word right and enjoyed the burst of laughter when he said it wrong. "Let's go to McDonald's and have hangoburs."

"We'll eat when we get home," said their father.

"In two hundred years," said Nicholas scathingly.

"There's tape in the first-aid kit, Dad," offered Langan. "We could seal his mouth."

"Don't tempt me."

The traffic in Hartford was terrible; the traffic in Hartford was always terrible. "Hartford," said Langan, "was designed by a cross-eyed Iraqi idiot."

Nicholas was thrilled. "Where?" he shouted, undoing his car-seat belt and pressing his nose up against the window.

"This," said Laura Mary Herrick gloomily, "is going to be a long war."

CHAPTER SEVEN

"About three-quarters of us are married," their father read from Mom's letter, "and most of the married personnel have children. So this is different from any other war, where only the young unmarried men go off to be killed. Nations don't mind killing their young men. I believe one reason we are holding off on ground war is that the lives of the soldiers count more than they used to. Nations don't mind if their nineteen-year-old boys die, but they don't like it when their thirty-something mothers and fathers die."

Langan was annoyed. Mom did not sound eager enough. He said grumpily, "I'd die in a heartbeat if that's what my country asked me to do."

His father grinned. "That's what she means. Teen-age boys all feel that way. If they don't mind, and their countries don't mind, what's the problem? Go for it. Wage war all century long."

"Dad! You sound like some protestor or some-thing."

"I'm not protesting. I'm not even arguing. If Pres-ident Bush says the way to get a better world is to smash Saddam Hussein, then I want to smash him too, Langan. But I want your mother home safe." He slopped peas onto everybody's plate, in spite of the fact that none of them liked peas. Langan knew he was doing it so he could write Mom that they were having vegetables.

"This is war," said Langan in vast disgust, as if he had waged thousands of them and knew more than anybody. "Nobody's safe."

Langan loves saying things like that, thought Laura. It sounds tough. He loves tough.

Dad read on, the bites of steak going slowly to his mouth, the letter propped against the salt shaker. "There are no discipline problems," wrote their mother. "Saudi Arabia does not allow alcohol, we are not near cities to acquire drugs, there are no prostitutes, or anything else except sand and scorpi-ons. I see now that rotten behavior has to start from something. It is a lie that boredom starts bad behav-ior. We are bored, and nobody has done a thing. If

Vietnam was the druggie/boozy war, this is the sober war."

"Here's a photo of her," said Dad. He studied it longer than they wanted him to, until Nicky said, "You're not sharing, Daddy," and grabbed it, his little fingers grubbing up the edges of the snapshot.

Mom was standing on flat rocky-looking sand. The horizon stretched behind her with no landmarks, no nothing. She was sober, sunburned, and healthy. From under the helmet, a single lock bleached by the sun had escaped. An armored vest covered her desert camo, the same ugly pattern the officers who gave briefings on television wore. She was hung with equipment: gas mask, rifle, canteen, unknown bulges and containers. She stood with her feet spread and she looked every inch a soldier. Her figure was not visible. Not a man or a woman, just a member of the army.

Dad taped the photograph to the refrigerator. After a while he sat back down and continued reading. "They have wonderful watermelon here. The street vendor digs his knife in and lets you sample a slice before you buy. Their highways are spectacular. Make Interstate 95 look like somebody's driveway. And do they go fast! Just when you think you're going suicide speed, a taxi of Arabs sitting on each other's laps passes you."

"Maybe she'll let us go that fast when she gets

back," said Langan. "That would be a real thrill ride."

Laura wondered how Mommy would come back. A soldier who drove at suicide speed among Arabs, silently folding socks in the laundry room, so nobody else in the family was bothered by the chore? Would Mommy come back somebody they didn't even know?

Mom's gossip ran on. Luz was homesick, Jarall had missed his son's birth, and Starr was upsetting the Saudi soldiers. "Starr says if the Saudis were keeping black people down the way they keep their women down, the United States wouldn't stand for it. The sergeant says, 'Starr, can we fight one war at a time please?' But Starr says she can fight twelve wars at a time any day of the week."

They lived for her letters. But even though Mom wrote good ones, Laura hated them. She didn't want Mommy to have a life of her own someplace else. She hated Mommy sounding busy and interested and even happy. Then she hated herself for feeling that way. Laura could not seem to feel good about anything. Sometimes she missed feeling good even more than she missed her mother. And the family could not seem to feel good either. It was as if Mom had been the engine and they were just pieces of car and couldn't roll without her.

"The desert's not like sand. Think talcum powder. At least that's the sand at our camp. We were in another part of the desert the other day and the sand there was more like gravel. We have to take our compasses with us wherever we go in case we get lost in a sandstorm. But there's nowhere to go, so it isn't a problem."

"She thinks *she* has nowhere to go," said Dad grumpily, staring around. Laundry baskets ringed the dinner table like an enemy siege. Nobody could believe how the laundry multiplied, as if hundreds of invisible people lived there, madly dirtying jeans and socks.

Mom may change, thought Laura, but Dad won't. He'll do some of these chores because he's the only one here, but he won't get good at them. Holding up the homefront does not count.

The phone rang. Dad was closest, but he could let a phone ring forever and not go near it. Neither Langan nor Laura could stand this habit. By the second ring, they were both vaulting over the furniture in the rush to answer it first. It turned out to be a questionable victory. "Hi, Grandma," said Langan sadly.

He looked longingly at his father, to hand the phone over, but Dad had become extremely busy cutting Nicholas's meat up for him. Nicholas loved knives and loved cutting his own meat, especially when the newly cut piece flew across the table. Nicky was grabbing his father's wrist, the knife handle, and the knife blade, trying to get a turn.

"Yes, we saw the news," said Langan. "But that doesn't mean war is going to start any minute, Grandma. It's nowhere near January fifteenth."

The United Nations and the allied forces and President Bush had given Iraq a deadline: either Saddam Hussein got out of Kuwait by January 15 or they would "use force" to kick him out.

Force! There were now over four hundred thousand American and allied troops in Saudi Arabia, lined up against Saddam.

"They'll go in ahead of that," said his grandmother darkly. "Mark my words, Langan."

"No, they won't, Grandma. The United Nations is going to give Saddam time to go home. And even when January fifteenth comes, it doesn't mean that President Bush is going to start firing guns at midnight plus thirty seconds. And even if he does, it doesn't mean that Mom is on the firing line. She's probably a thousand miles away pumping gas into some general's Jeep."

"Well, here in Conyers' Pond, we're sure they'll go in before the deadline," said Grandma. "Your poor, poor mother."

Conyers' Pond. The Herrick and the Forsey families had a real ability to pick residences in the hick backwaters of the United States. Langan did not intend to do this. Langan was going to live someplace that mattered. New York or Los Angeles.

"Furthermore, if she's pumping gas for generals,"

added his grandmother, "she's not safe at all. The generals are where the action is."

It was a miracle to Langan that Rosalys had come out of her family sane. No wonder she taught kindergarten. She was probably trying to make up for all the Grandma Forsey types damaging their kids with all their depressing talk. "There's no action," said Langan firmly. "Stop worrying, Grandma. How's Bingo? You guys win much lately?" His grandparents adored Bingo, and played several nights a week. Along with not living in the boonies when he grew up, Langan planned never to spend time with people who gloated over things like "B 6" or "I 22."

Langan discussed peace with his grandmother. The last thing Langan wanted was peace, of course. He wanted war, lots of war, splashy, exciting, thrilling war, that he would watch on TV and would last long enough for him to get into it and win medals and drive a tank.

But even though the war was popular and everybody at Wash was thrilled about it, still it wasn't good form to rub your hands together with glee. You had to talk peace, even though your heart was with war.

Langan's heart confused him.

At the same time that war was like a race car zooming around the track, revving its engine and roaring toward the finish line, he wanted to be the driver or at least have a front-row seat for the race—he was filled with anxiety. Anxiety shuddered in his gut the way he supposed ulcers did. Walking around like little feet trying to find a dry place to stand in all that stomach acid.

In gym for six weeks they were in the weight room. The school had a treadmill, and Langan had had his first chance on it. He was off almost immediately. "Too hard, huh?" said the instructor, grinning savagely. The gym instructor loved to give them stuff that was too hard, too heavy, too dangerous.

But the treadmill was not too hard for his legs; it was too hard for his mind. It was like home: a nightmarish running in place, without ever getting anywhere, without ever quite having your life in order, because the orderly part of it was gone.

Langan was not a fan of order. The worst thing in his life was being forced to clean his room. When he had a house of his own, he used to tell Rosalys, he would never clean. Never neaten. Never make lists. Well, he had that kind of house now, and it was lousy. Last Saturday Dad grimly made everybody vacuum, scrub, dust, or fold, and the house reached a sort of truce with its own mess, but did not actually become orderly.

Langan marveled at the power of the house itself to take over their lives. How had Mom controlled the house? What were her secrets?

Christmas was coming. A holiday took more order than anything. They were going to have a terrible Christmas. And what would even be the point of celebrating? Mom was gone.

Langan's chest filled with a queer pain. The coach ordered him back on the treadmill and he hiked, getting nowhere except closer and closer to tears.

Nicholas was intolerable.

When he and Dad got home at six-fifteen, cranky was not the word. Nicholas demanded to be held straight till bedtime, being read to, sung to, played with. You stopped, he screamed. He sounded like an ambulance siren, not a human being. Every time you said you weren't going to give in, you gave in.

He knew the magic words, and they were not *please* or *thank you*. They were *I miss Mommy*!

"Maybe we should communicate with Saddam Hussein," said Langan to his father, who looked at Langan wearily.

"Saddam," said Langan, pointing to Nicky, "have we got a target for you."

They managed a laugh.

Laura was wearing her little brother like a preppie's sweater: his body draped on her back, arms linked beneath Laura's chin. "Let's ship Nicky to Grandma and Grandpa for the duration," suggested Laura.

Nicky took her seriously. "I'll be good, Laura," he

said fearfully, slipping off her back. "I'll be good," he said again, swerving around to find proof that he was worth keeping. He retrieved an abandoned ice-cream dish sitting half over the edge of the TV shelf and carried it to the sink. "Can I stay?"

"She was joking, buddy," said Dad. He scooped Nicholas up and tumbled him around, like laundry. But nobody laughed. "Okay," said their father. "Okay." He seemed to be answering somebody's order. He roused himself with a tremendous effort. "Somebody get a pencil. We need to make a Christmas list."

Laura loved Christmas lists. Where there were lists, there was hope.

"Tree," dictated Dad. "Wreath. Stocking presents. Turkey. Candy."

"Chain saw," said Langan, also full of hope.

"Over my dead body," said his father.

Nicholas screamed.

The family stared at him. He climbed up Laura like a jungle gym and hung on tight enough to strangle. "Nicky," she said irritably.

"They couldn't both die, could they?" said Nicholas. "Both dead? Laura, you won't die, will you? Let's not anybody die."

"How beautiful the desert sky is at night," wrote their mother. "Billions more stars here in the desert than at home. Or maybe I never took the time to look up at home.

"And camels. Up close—scruffy and ridiculous. But from a distance, elegant. We see them all the time on the horizon. I think of Baby Jesus and wise men. Are you getting ready for Christmas? Do you realize we will not be together for Christmas? I am counting on you to do Christmas right for my sake. I don't know how we will do Christmas in an Arab country, but Starr says at least we will have the best manger scene in the world."

His father had just finished shaving and had gone to get dressed when Nicholas decided he wanted a sip of water. There were no paper cups left in the bathroom and his plastic mug was full of soap scum from being used as a tub toy, so Nicholas went down to the kitchen sink. His big sister was upstairs choosing and rejecting clothing combinations. His big brother was out in the garage patting the snow thrower. Nicholas got a clean glass out of the dishwasher and climbed up on the counter to reach the tap.

He lost his balance.

Nicholas, the glass, and Langan's breakfast dishes fell backward onto the hard tile floor.

Screams were so routine from Nicky that his family probably wouldn't have come just for screams; it was the sound of breaking glass that brought his sister and father running. He'd cut himself all down one arm. Band-Aids were not enough; he was going to need stitches.

Laura wrapped his arm tightly in a dish towel. "We'll have to take him to the emergency clinic."

Her father was shaking. He hardly even looked at the cut. "I cannot be late to work!" he bellowed, slamming his briefcase against the wall. His breathing was uneven and out of control. "The bank is sending out layoff notices like bowling balls!" he shouted. "You want me to be late? You want me to lose my job? How do you want me to pay all the bills? Huh? Answer me that?"

"I'm sorry, Daddy," whispered Nicky, whose breath was also shuddering. He pressed tight against the safety of Laura.

Laura stood very still, willing her father to regain control.

Dad took a very deep breath. "It's okay, honey," he said shakily to his son. "It was an accident. It isn't your fault. Daddy just has to try to think what to do next. Oh, Laura, why aren't you old enough to drive?"

Dad called Mrs. Schwann, Ellen's mother, who agreed reluctantly to take Nicky to the clinic for him, although clearly she felt any decent sort of father would be doing this himself. Laura made a note never to swim in Ellen Schwann's pool again. Laura taped the dish towel with Scotch tape and

Dad dropped Nicky at the Schwanns on his frantic way to the bank.

Langan, of course, had slipped out of the house like a weasel: a quick, skinny, unreliable little rodent. Oh, sometimes Laura hated her brothers! Why couldn't Langan pitch in on anything? Why was it always her?

Blood, glass, milk, cereal, and dirty underwear covered the floor.

She picked up Nicholas's cereal bowl and changed her mind about putting it in the dishwasher. Instead she flung it at the wall. It shattered in a dozen small shards, which spread around the kitchen like shrapnel.

Great, she thought. Langan is a rodent, Daddy is having a nervous breakdown, Nicky needs stitches, and I'm smashing dishes.

Laura heard the distinctive diesel-y sound of her own school bus leaving without her.

Couldn't call Mrs. Schwann; she was clinic-bound with Nicky. She called Hope and Johanna's mother.

"Laura, dear," said Mrs. Randell, "I'm afraid you're going to have to work a little bit harder at keeping the family going. You owe it to your mother, Laura. Try to take some responsibility."

Try to take some responsibility?

Maybe she would walk to school. It was only four miles. Only take her two hours. Probably get kidnapped on the way. But that was better than owing Mrs. Randell a favor.

"Your mother might die for her country," pointed out Mrs. Randell, "and what are you doing? Missing the school bus."

Laura thought it would be nice if Mrs. Randell died for her country.

"But of course I'll be delighted to drive you," said Mrs. Randell.

Laura wanted to know how come the woman had named a daughter Hope? Why not Viper?

Laura got to school late and within the hour received a summons to the guidance office. The minute she walked into the room she knew this was no late-to-school lecture. The room was packed: her own class adviser, the school psychologist, and two people Laura did not even know.

"Laura, you're the only child in our school with a parent in Saudi Arabia, and we want to make sure your family is coping all right."

Coping? thought Laura. We're not even speaking. We're drowning in dirty clothes and all we have for Christmas is a list.

"We could have a visiting nurse stop in, you know. And of course, if you need counseling, we're always here for you."

I'm a prisoner of war, thought Laura. The enemy is interrogating me. But I am strong. I will not let my father down. "We're fine. We haven't had any problems. We're a military family and we expect this kind of thing." Laura was quite pleased with how easily she lied. She did not do much lying, but clearly this had been an error. Lying to a pack of shrinks was fun.

"Nobody's depressed or overly upset?" The school psychologist was eager. She wanted a little depression to handle. She wanted Laura to say bad things about how her father was managing. Laura would die first.

"We're coping well," Laura said politely. She countered every question without revealing a thing and went back to class feeling triumphant and brave. We have met the enemy, she thought, and survived.

But she had to sit next to Jan, who found time to tell Laura what fun it was to date Kenneth, and how amused Jan and Kenneth had been that Laura asked Kenneth out. "We laughed so hard," said Jan. "Didn't we, Kenny-kens?"

Kenny-kens?

These were the times when you could see how an M-16 would come in handy.

"I'm writing to Mom," said Dad, waving an airmail envelope at them. "You guys write too, and you do a good drawing on airmail paper, Nicky." He passed out sheets of onionskin paper.

"I'll do a Teenage Mutant Ninja Turtle," said

Nicholas eagerly, but when he bore down on the thin paper it ripped, and he burst into tears. "I need real paper!" he cried.

"I'll give you another sheet of this paper," said Dad. "Just try to be careful."

"I'm being careful," shouted Nicky. He grabbed his second sheet fiercely and accidentally crumpled it in his hot little fist. He was much too clumsy for paper as fragile as airmail paper. Laura could have suggested that they just pay more postage and let Nicky use construction paper, but that would lead to the am-I-made-of-money? argument.

Laura and Langan withdrew to their bedrooms to write their letters.

She's always asking how we're doing, thought Laura. So I'll start with that.

Dear Mommy, she planned. We're not doing so good. It turns out there is nothing on earth that can't set Nicky off and also make Daddy mad. You were the river we floated on, Mommy, and now we're grounded and can't get off the raft. We all half hate coming home because you're not here, and you're not here in so many ways! You're not here to keep us calm, or cook supper, or smell of your perfume, or stop Langan when he's being worthless. You're so completely *not here*.

She didn't write that down. She got up and turned on the radio instead and danced for a while.

* * *

Dear Mom, Langan planned to write, it's really fun in school with you gone. Everybody says how terrific I am because my mother is a soldier. I'm more popular than I've ever been. In fact, now that I know what popular is, I don't think I've *been* popular before. What I hope is, you're gone long enough for this to stick. I mean, I don't want my popularity to run out when you come home. So don't feel you have to rush.

He didn't write that down. He got up and turned on the radio instead.

So okay, thought Laura, I won't write about what's going on at home. Which leaves school. She's always interested in school.

Dear Mommy, planned Laura. It's the pits in school with you gone. Everybody is so interested in me. I feel like a science exhibit. Especially in guidance, they want to know if we're having problems. See, they want to be involved in the war effort too, and they figure that helping us past our difficulties will be their contribution. Of course we are having approximately a million difficulties, mostly Daddy's. But I can't tell on him. Meanwhile, the one person I want to have interested in me, namely Kenneth, is interested in Jan. If Saddam Hussein doesn't have enough victims to go around, he can have Jan.

Laura didn't write that down. She changed radio

stations several times, found nothing fabulous, and put in a cassette instead.

Langan played tic-tac-toe with himself for some time. I'm a skunk. I like popularity more than I miss Mom.

He had a vision of himself as one of those heartless, cold, inhuman horrors who turn out to be mass murderers.

I do love you, Mom, he thought. I do. I want you to be safe. I miss you. But I love being important and special.

"Dear Mom," Langan wrote at last. "So how are you? I am fine. Nothing is happening here."

Laura arranged her cassette tapes alphabetically by performer. Finally she picked up her pen again and wrote, "Dear Mom. So how are you? I am fine. Nothing is happening here."

Laura lined the Christmas box they were sending Mom with green tissue paper that had sparkles all over it. There wasn't much room in the box and they didn't want to send anything she wouldn't want. This was not the kind of Christmas for stuff like cute earrings. So far they had three magazines of crossword puzzles, six medieval English romances they knew she loved, Gummie Bears, a little bottle of perfume, and Nicky's artwork from day care. A Charlie Daniels cassette, to make her homesick, and a cassette recording of the four of them at breakfast, to make her glad she was in Saudia Arabia. Clippings from the local newspaper (Mom being a devoted gossip), especially City Legals, which were house sales, divorce filings, and lawsuits brought against neighbors. Shawnee had found an eight-inch Christmas tree made from real evergreens for Langan to send, and Laura had hung it with tiny silver bells that really jangled.

Laura tried to think Christmas thoughts. They didn't come. Her entire brain was folded up in war and soldiers and gas masks. It was like being addicted: she could not wrench her thoughts away. Even Kenneth, even Jan, could keep her attention only for moments, and then she was sucked back into war thoughts.

Laura hoped that the desert this year was full of wise men. That they would guide and protect her mother. At least they have something better than camels to do it with, she thought.

"Let's put in some mistletoe," said Langan. "She can hang it in the tent door and all the guys can kiss her."

Laura looked at him. "You think Dad wants that?"

"Oh yeah. I forgot. She's married, huh?"

"Yeah, well, neither of *them* better forget it," said Laura.

"This is true," said her brother. Laura looked at Langan. Langan looked at Laura.

They hadn't actually liked each other in years. The smile between them was small, but it was real.

At the basketball game, the starters for the opposing team were introduced, and the fans for that side cheered, whistled, and stomped. Then the home team was introduced, and the fans for that side cheered, whistled, and stomped. Laura and the rest of the cheerleaders did splits and jumps and rustled their pompons.

Then everybody stood up for *The Star-Spangled Banner*.

Usually this was simply a portion of the game ritual that lasted too long. Nobody ever sang the national anthem anymore. People just stood, bored, on the bleachers, waiting for it to end. The last several beats were always interrupted by applause and screaming for the game to begin.

The spectators waited for the cassette to play.

Most schools had a band, or a trumpeter at the least, but Laura's school had a lousy music program and a tape was the best they could do. It wasn't even a good tape. It scratched a lot.

Silence.

Everybody stood still.

More silence.

The scorekeeper picked up his mike. "I apologize. The tape seems to be broken. We'll skip the anthem and go straight to the game."

Laura had been to basketball games every winter of her life: hundreds of them. The crowd would now sit down, kids snickering, adults yawning, glad to skip the nuisance of the tedious anthem.

But the crowd remained standing.

Looking silently at the flag on the far wall.

Nobody sat down.

From the student end of the gym, high on the bleachers where the worst kids sat—kids whose swearing made refs give a technical to the other team—a single shaky boy's voice began. "O say can you see, by the dawn's early light . . ."

Laura's whole body prickled.

The rest of the students joined in. ". . . what so proudly we hailed . . ."

The families, the coaches, the cheerleaders, and finally even the starters out on the court began to sing too.

Laura would have bet half the people didn't even know the words. She would have been wrong. *The Star-Spangled Banner* gathered force and strength, filling the gym with such emotion that Laura had to cover her eyes. *Oh, Mommy, they're singing this for you.*

And when the song ended, and the cheering began, it was not for the game.

It was for the flag.

CHAPTER EIGHT

"It's Mommy!" screamed Nicholas, waving the phone so frantically he banged it into the wall and dropped it. "Mommy!" he screamed toward the phone on the floor.

Langan and Laura made flying leaps for the fallen phone.

Heads banged on walls and other heads. Muffled curses and moans of pain filled the air.

Their mother's laugh came over the wire. "Hi, guys," she said. "I guess nothing's changed, huh?"

Laura got it. "Oh, Mom!" she said. And then again, "Oh, Mom!"

"Hi, honey. How's it going?"

"We're fine, we're absolutely fine. How are you?"

"I'm fine, just fine."

Laura could think of nothing else to say. She just wanted her mother's voice to continue.

"I got your last care package," said her mother. "Thank you so much for sending me cookies. Everybody else is getting dumb stuff like Chap Stick or suntan lotion. That's issued to us. It's so dumb to be mailing that. But I was the only one to get cookies. Homemade cookies. From my daughter."

"Had they crumbled?" said Laura anxiously.

"Completely. We had such fun, licking the box and our fingers, doling out the chocolate chips like lottery tickets. It was yummy, Laura."

Laura tried to imagine Starr and Mom, passing a cardboard box around and licking the corners. While gas masks bumped on their chests.

"Merry Christmas, Mommy," said Laura.

Until this moment the tree had just been a green thing in the living room, the presents just boxes, and the turkey in the oven just food. Now suddenly the room was warm, and loving, and good. The season was here and the joy was alive. "I love you, Mommy," she said, and handed the phone quickly to Nicholas before she began sobbing out of control.

"Did you get my pictures, Mommy?" Nicholas beamed at his mother's answer. He said, exclusively to his father, as if Langan and Laura were not home, "She stapled my pictures right onto the tent right over her cot. So there." Nicholas, having learned what counted, handed the phone to his father and went back to the television.

Television news was more real to him than his mother's voice.

The television was more real than his mother's life.

What are we doing to Nicky? thought Laura. We have to turn the television off. We have to do little-boy stuff like we used to—like Mom used to, any-way. I have to take Nicky to the park, and the library story hour, and the science museum. Langan has to throw him a ball in the backyard again. Daddy has to take him on thrill rides.

"We're doing fine, I guess," said her father. "We're a little tired. I'm not the list maker I'd like to be."

Laura suddenly realized that she was disap-pointed in her father. Thrill rides he could handle, but the daily grind—he just didn't want it. This list excuse was nonsense. If he wanted the house to run right, he'd run it right. A man who could run a bank could run a home.

He's mad because these are Mommy's jobs, thought Laura. He's making it not work. He could get up half an hour earlier to dress Nicky on time. He'd rather screw it up than take it over.

Her father looked at the Christmas tree, which they had forced themselves to decorate only last night. "We miss you," he said huskily. "Keep your head down, chickadee."

Langan looked at his father. "Chickadee" was a term of endearment that always softened Mom up. Langan did not know where it came from. Suddenly he was immensely proud. One parent was a warrior and one kept the faith; he did not have a divorce in his family and his father was making it work no matter what the odds were.

Langan detested the word "love" and all the baggage that went with it. He did not use the word with his tongue or in his head. He did not use it now. But his heart swelled, and when his father bent over the phone, eyes full of tears, Langan would have done anything on earth he was asked to do.

Luckily nobody knew, and the moment passed safely.

"How is everybody letting off steam?" said Dad, wearing his casual voice, the one that meant he was nervous. This was not a private question, so Langan and Laura put their heads up close to the phone so they could listen along. Nicholas stayed with the television.

"There's no beer," said Mom, "so we don't relax on booze. This is going to be the world's biggest drying-out program. We play volleyball. Softball, sometimes, but it's tougher to mix sexes. We could rig only one basketball hoop so we had to change the rules. Everybody's reading thrillers. Somebody found a stray dog and we spend a lot of time loving her up. Starr got homemade doughnuts the other day, hard as rocks, but everybody wanted one, so we ran relay races to see who got doughnuts."

"You sound pretty cheerful."

"I am, actually. It's essential, Tag. This one girl, she's only nineteen, her fiancé's in Saudi Arabia somewhere, but she can't find him, and she has no parents and nobody has written to her—she started crying last week and it took the whole unit to get her propped up again. So we don't let ourselves get down."

"I'm down," said Dad suddenly. It was an admission they could never have expected. The pain broke through on his face, and Laura bled for him.

"Don't come apart," said Mom, her voice coming apart at her end. "I know you're doing a perfect job. Don't let go, Tag. I love you. Merry Christmas."

"I love you," he said, his words swamped in guilt. They were not doing a perfect job. Especially he was not doing a perfect job. And it was not a merry Christmas. He gave Laura the phone. "Goodbye, Mommy," cried Laura, "keep calling. Call us all the time." She was blurry with emotion. Her mother's final words rang like silver bells in her ears. "I love you, Laura."

"Merry Christmas, Mommy. Stay alert!"

Nicholas wasn't even listening to add his line,

"The world needs more lerts." He was squatting in front of the TV, holding his ankles and rocking like a blond toad.

Laura tried to keep the warmth of the phone call inside herself, but it evaporated the instant the connection ceased. She wanted Mommy at home, playing kindergarten teacher, making them sing *Rudolph* and *Santa Claus Is Coming* and *The First Noel*.

After a while she became aware of a loud rhythmic clanging from outside the house. "What's that, Langan?"

Her brother frowned. "Dad must be splitting wood."

They had not used the wood stove yet this winter. Wood stoves were a royal pain and a humongous mess if you didn't do it right and do it constantly. Life this winter had so many other humongous pains that adding the wood stove had been too much.

Langan looked out the kitchen door but couldn't see his father. He slid around the corner of the house. Dad was not just splitting the logs in halves, and then quarters. He was turning the logs into splinters. Into kindling. Whaling the wood with a ferocity like homicide.

Langan slid back behind the house again.

If Mom had died, he thought, or divorced us, Dad wouldn't have a problem. He'd just do it all. But now . . . She's the soldier and he stirs the spaghetti sauce. She has the classified position and he has the detergent.

Langan went back inside.

His sister was doing a girl thing—folding ropes of pine needles around candles in the middle of the table. Langan marveled, as always, at the things girls spent time on. "What's happening?" said his sister.

"Mom's the warrior," said Langan briefly.

He and his sister set the table for Christmas dinner. It was so awful setting just four places that for a moment he considered setting a fifth anyway. Would it be too weird and upsetting to have an empty plate and glass and unfolded napkin at Mommy's place?

Langan actually had a moment in which he wished Grandma and Grandpa had come down, so they would have more people. Then he caught himself.

On TV a female GI sauntered across a wide expanse of hard sand to a row of plywood doors. Just doors, all by themselves. No buildings. Flinging one open, she stepped in, shut the door, and piece by piece draped her clothing over the door. Then her small black hand reached up to turn a faucet, and water sprayed down.

The woman was taking her shower out in the middle of the desert in front of the cameras of the world.

"Mom would hate that," said Laura. Suddenly

she was terribly angry that any of this was happening. Interfering with people's lives and Christmases and showers. "How come nobody else is in this war with us?" said Laura darkly.

"Everybody else is," Nicholas contradicted her.

"What do *you* know?" demanded his big sister. She looked at him with un-Christmasy scorn.

"I know everything," said Nicholas calmly. "Britain has Zeros."

They stared at him. "Where is Britain?" said Langan, being mean and testing a four-year-old's geography.

"In Saudi Arabia, dummy," said Nicholas. "With their Zeros."

The following week, the temperature finally, finally, finally began to fall to normal winter depths. There was talk of snow. Snow was going to fall.

Snow, beautiful, blessed snow!

And this was Friday! Which meant he didn't even have to worry about school interfering with his driveways! He could throw snow all day Saturday, probably end up with fifty driveways, instead of twenty-two! He'd have the cash to pay the Sears bill by lunchtime!

Langan could hardly sleep for thinking of how deep it would be, and how he would use his powerful snow thrower and make lots of money. He'd show everybody a thing or two. Shawnee and Astle and everybody at school thought he couldn't do anything right. His own father had sworn at him and tried to make him return the snow thrower and said they were going to be out eight hundred dollars because of Langan's stupidity.

Well, he'd be out there making his first million and then they'd see.

Langan slept at last, gathering strength for the first voyage of the snow thrower in the first snow of a fabulous year.

Just before dawn the snow turned to rain.

By the time Langan was up, it had turned to slush, deep and ugly.

No snow thrower could move slush. Too wet. Too heavy.

Twenty-two driveways.

He had not ever considered what he would do without the snow thrower's help. His driveways were in a spiffy little subdivision called Windermere. Each driveway was aimed at a two-car garage, with a sophisticated curve in the blacktop and extra parking areas for the third car and the guests. The driveways were in excellent condition, smooth . . . and big.

At 7:00 A.M. Langan put on boots, heavy coat, wool cap, and thick gloves. He wondered how long it would be before the rain soaked through them.

He walked down to Windermere and inspected

the first driveway. The slush would have to be ladled off, like soup. One heavy shovelful at a time.

Just like everybody had told him, back when they said he didn't know what he was doing.

The owner came out. "Kid? You the one said he was going to plow?"

"Yes, sir."

"Better get going. It's gonna freeze tonight. I don't wanna come home to ice all over my driveway. Hear me?"

Langan swallowed. "Yes, sir." He walked home and got the snow shovel out of the garage, walked back to Windermere, and got started. The first driveway took him twenty-five minutes. The slush just slurped off the shovel. At the end of two hours he had done only seven of his twenty-two driveways. His back ached, his hands were frozen, his boots were soaked through, and the rain on the back of his neck had become an ice scarf. Nine in the morning and he was practically a corpse.

I have to get this done, he thought. I am not going to have anybody say *I told you so*.

Langan leaned momentarily on the shovel handle, trying not to think about how much his back hurt.

Across the street, somebody else was shoveling one of his driveways.

It was his father. "Hey, kid," said Dad, shoveling to meet him.

Langan was afraid he would cry or give his father a kiss or something, so he said, "Where'd you get the shovel?" They had only one.

"Bought it half an hour ago," said his father. "On sale at the hardware store. We can always use another one, huh?"

Just when you thought you couldn't count on somebody, you could count on him. "Meet you in the middle," said Langan.

CHAPTER NINE

The United Nations had agreed that Saddam Hussein should move his little body and his half million troops out of Kuwait by January 15.

Saddam Hussein had not agreed.

Saddam Hussein, far from moving out, had dug in, filling the sand for a million miles with a million land mines.

On the other side of the line in the sand—the Saudi Arabian side—Americans, Egyptians, British, Saudis, French, and Syrians were prepared for the largest, most technologically advanced war the world had ever seen.

On his side, Saddam Hussein had the Republican Guards, his best: lethal shock troops who would slash through battle leaving nothing but blood in their wake.

As the days rushed toward January 15, Laura's heart seemed to rush also: her pulse was faster, her breathing shorter and shallower.

Where was Mommy? Where was the 333rd?

What were those horrible Scud missiles of Saddam Hussein's that everybody talked about: those terrible monsters that slicked through the sky and dropped anywhere, killing everything?

But Tuesday, January 15, was just Tuesday.

Just school, no big deal.

Of course they talked about the deadline in every class, but it didn't feel *there*.

And it wasn't there. Everybody slept tight on Tuesday and went to school again on Wednesday and came home and that was that.

Daddy had taken off as soon as the bank closed at three and brought Nicky home. When Laura and Langan got in, Daddy was already in his big heavy chair in front of the television. He seemed embarrassed to be home. "I feel in my bones nothing is going to happen," he said quickly. "I just wanted to be near the news. In case something does. Although I'm sure something won't. It's impossible to have a war so programmed, like a Nintendo game."

"Let's buy a Nintendo," said Nicholas immediately.

"No," said Langan, not referring to Nintendo. "The troops and the ships and the pilots are ready, Dad. Four hundred thousand men and women are ready. Toes edging the starting line. Adrenaline pumping." Langan shook his head. "No, they're go. I promise you, Dad. General Colin Powell's gonna kick ass sooner, not later."

They took their positions in front of the TV.

Daddy had his huge chair, and Nicholas had either Daddy's lap or the floor and his Legos. Nicholas said, "I'm gonna build a Scud with my Legos. What do they look like, Daddy?"

"Long and thin," said Dad. "Like a pencil."

"Not mine," said Nicholas. "Mine has nails all over it and two million hundred bombs coming out the sides."

Langan had the sofa, on which he lay lengthwise, taking up the whole thing. Laura usually sat on a floor pillow, with her back propped up against the sofa. One of the drawbacks was smelling Langan's feet.

"If I were Bush I'd be sneaky," said Langan, who loved to imagine himself as the commander in chief. "Let the guy think I'm really a wuss and I'm not going to do anything. Minute it's dark in Iraq, I'd let him have it."

"But they have special glasses to see in the dark with," objected Laura. "They can see fine no matter when we go. They'll see us. Shoot us down. Kill our pilots!"

It was to be an air war. Americans and allies were to pound them—assuming anything was done at all, which nobody seemed sure of—from the air only, hitting military targets, headquarters, munitions storage, and bridges. The U.S. wouldn't go in with ground troops and tanks till the planes had dented up Iraqi defenses. Of course, then the troops would run into those Republican Guards, who were ten times as mean and savage as anybody in America had ever thought of being.

Mommy's been gone for eight weeks now, thought Laura.

Eight weeks. It was impossible.

They watched television hour after hour.

People were worried about whether Israel would sit tight. It was not Israel's kind of thing, sitting tight.

For Laura, Israel was mostly Bethlehem, and the manger at Christmas.

She knew that in modern times, Israel was a Jewish state, a tough crowd who had put their country together, and held it together, against the violent threats of the immense surrounding Arab countries, who hated their guts. Her father loved the Israelis. He loved their guts. He said Israel could whip every Arab in town with their hands tied behind their backs. Her father had tremendous respect for power.

Part of Saddam Hussein's strategy would be to show the world he could kick Israel around at last.

If Saddam could bring Israel in, if he bombed Jerusalem and Tel Aviv, the Israelis would fight back, and the Arab countries who hated Israel would switch sides, join up with Saddam, pulverize Israel . . . and America too.

Rosalys Herrick. Starr. Jarral. Luz. David. All the 333rd.

Laura worried and worried. There were too many ways for it to go. Her mind leaped from one bloody scenario to another, and her heart leaped after the blood like frogs smacking their lily pads. She knew there were almost half a million families as nervous as she was—but she didn't feel any better.

Israel wasn't Langan's worry. Israel knew how to take care of itself. Langan's worry was that the USA would not attack at all but just sit in the sand like a whipped dog.

As the U.S. correspondent in Israel spoke, the Connecticut lottery numbers appeared on the screen. It offended Laura. It was cheap, mixing war with lottery tickets.

The commentator said that there were now 430,000 American troops in the Gulf.

"How many is four hundred thirty thousand, Daddy?" said Nicholas.

"A lot."

"Show me," said Nicholas.

"Come sit on my lap. We'll make four hundred thirty thousand marks on a piece of paper."

"By the time you get that done, war will have started," said Langan, giving his father a notebook. Dad propped it against his knees and began making sets of four vertical lines crossed by the fifth. "Five," said Dad.

"Five," agreed Nicholas happily.

"Ten. Fifteen. Twenty. Twenty-five. Thirty." They arranged that Dad would make the four up and down marks, but Nicky would make the cross hatch. It was going to be a game of which Nicholas would never tire.

On ABC, Peter Jennings was walking from country to country on an immense floor map, the tips of his shoes at riverbanks and mountain ranges, his stride taking him from Kuwait to Jordan, from Syria to Saudi Arabia. Laura liked the map. She could figure out the action on that map.

Laura was starving. And she did not want to cook. She hated cooking. Daddy and Langan would skip supper rather than take their turns. "Daddy, let's order pizza."

He looked unbelievably tired, and he and Nicky had reached only five hundred. "I don't have the cash, sweetie."

"Don't stop, Daddy," ordered Nicky in his high, clear voice.

Laura opened the freezer.

The ABC reporter live in Baghdad—capital of Iraq, home of Saddam Hussein—said, "Wait. Something's happening. I see something in the sky."

Laura sure didn't see anything in the freezer. A box of frozen squash that had probably been there since last winter. Fat-free ice cream, too disgusting even for Nicholas to eat. An open bag of Tater Tots and a pudding pop covered with ice crystals.

"It looks like fireworks," said the reporter on ABC.

"Laura," said her father.

"There's nothing in the freezer, Dad. But we've got a ham slice."

"Something's happening!" said the reporter.

"I hate ham," said Nicholas.

"Nobody cares about you," said Langan.

"I want French toast," said Nicholas.

"Okay," said Laura. "Stale bread we've got."

"Laura, look at the TV," said her father. He was sitting up, eyes wide, fingers stiffly splayed on the chair arms.

The screen was black. A row of white dots glittered along the lower center and a bunch of white dots sparkled on and off in the upper portion.

"Baghdad," whispered her father, wetting his lips.

It didn't look like Baghdad to Laura. It looked like they had lost the cable connection.

Baghdad must be an awful place to be female. Imagine wearing those long black gowns, your face always covered. If you were nearsighted did you get to wear glasses? What about your hair? It would always be messed up.

"Tracer fire. Huge red tracers!" said the reporter. The know-it-all blankness of voice that every television reporter cultivated had disappeared. This guy was both shrieking and choking.

"It's begun!" shouted Langan, pounding fist into palm. "Right on schedule! This is great!" He leaped into the air and came down with a thud, smashing several Legos under his work boots.

"Pound the bastards, Mom!" shouted Langan. "Kick ass! Level the place! Pave it!"

"I don't know what's happening," shouted the reporter feverishly, "but it's happening!"

Articulate, thought Laura. Must have hired him for his understanding of deep and complex problems. Laura opened the fridge and began sorting through abandoned containers. Plenty of eggs. They could have ham omelets. And toast with jam.

"Who's shooting who?" shouted Nicky.

"We're shooting them!" shouted Langan.

"Yay!" screamed Nicky.

Dad switched to CNN. CNN's reporter yelled, "Whoa! Holy cow! That was a large airburst!"

Laura found two onions and half a wrinkled-up old green pepper to throw into the omelets.

"Those are bombs," said Nicholas. "TV said so. Pow!" he added happily. "Kill 'em, huh, Langan?"

"You got it, my man," said his big brother.

Laura heated the large cast-iron skillet.

"Saddam Hussein!" yelled Langan, in a voice loud enough to reach New York, if not Baghdad. "You're toasted now, buddy!"

What am I doing? thought Laura Herrick. War has started and I'm whipping up an omelet? Get a grip, girl.

She let the whisk fall into the egg bowl. She took the heavy pillow off the sofa, shoveled away a few thousand Legos with her shoe, plopped the pillow on the floor, and sat.

The spokesman for the White House came on. "The liberation of Kuwait has begun," he said.

Laura felt a queer sick prickle all over.

Dad sat on the very edge of his heavy chair. He hardly blinked or breathed. When he reached out for his beer, his hand closed on Langan's strawberry soda instead. He didn't notice the difference. If he spoke, it was whispered, as if the conversation were between him and the war. "Get the bastards!" he whispered twice, as huge showers of explosions filled the Baghdad sky.

The broadcasting went on and on, with experts on one channel and experts on other channels. You couldn't really see anything except blackness and white sprinkles.

Nobody was calling it Desert Shield anymore: that was the code word for prewar. Now it was Desert Storm.

It doesn't feel like war, thought Laura.

Her appetite was the only thing killed so far.

But I don't know that, thought Laura. Other women's children might be dead right now. Out in those Baghdad streets. They can't all jump out of the way.

She wondered if you could see a bomb coming. Was it like tornadoes in Kansas, where there was time to gather the children and run to the cellar? She imagined herself in a heavy, black, eye-slitted robe, as bombs and buildings fell on her and broke her bones and killed her children.

"I'm hungry," said Nicholas.

Dad did not react. Laura doubted if he even heard. Langan got up, muttering, "Don't take my place on the sofa, Laura," and opened a bag of Oreo cookies for Nicky.

"For *supper*?" said Nicholas. Then even Nicky knew enough to lie low, so Daddy didn't remember stuff like vegetables and fruit. He curled up at Laura's feet, staring at the popping firebursts on the dark TV screen and slurping cookies. Only Nicky could make so much noise on a dry cookie.

The correspondent in central Saudia Arabia flickered onto the screen. "Where Mommy is?" asked Nicholas. He had difficulty with the concept of maps.

"Where Mommy is," agreed their father. His eyes were fastened to the screen, as if he belonged to it, were partially within it.

"Well, everybody here is putting on gas masks," said the correspondent, looking around nervously. He had never had to cut off transmitting in order to don a gas mask. He looked unsure of the etiquette.

"What's a little nerve gas?" said Langan. "Hang in there, my man."

Where are you, Mommy? thought Laura. Are you out there in the dark, with things exploding around you? Is it cold on the sand? Are you scared? Are you waiting for them to shoot back? *Mommy. Be all right.*

The president spoke at 9:00 P.M. He looked less tired and old than he usually did. "While the world waited," he began.

"Too long," interrupted Langan, who thought they should have beaten Saddam Hussein into shape ages ago.

"No nation can break the law," said the president.

"Yeah," said Langan, "don't fuck with America."

"Langan, swear—and you're in your room listening to the radio, got it?" said his father.

"Got it," said Langan irritably.

143

"And?" shouted their father.

"And what?" said Langan insolently.

Their father's eyes left the television and he got up out of the chair.

We'll have our own war, thought Laura, he's gonna toast Langan.

"I'm sorry," said Langan quickly. "I won't swear again, Dad."

"Your mother hates that word. She's out there in a desert, fighting for this country, while you're breaking her rules here at home?"

Langan sat down. "I'm sorry."

"Stay sorry!"

"Okay, Dad."

The night went on and on. It was weirdly companionable, because you knew the entire nation was tucked up in front of their TV sets too, watching the same broadcasts and worrying about the same soldiers. Other people were eating what was handy, too, like Oreo cookies, because who could leave to fix anything else?

The secretary of defense came on. "I like him," said Langan. "I want him and Colin Powell to run for president."

"I thought you were so fond of the one we have," said Laura.

"I am. But I'm fonder of Colin Powell and Dick Cheney."

"But what's really happening?" said Nicholas. "I can't really see very well."

"Nobody can see very well," said Dad. "That's the night sky over Baghdad, and most of the explosions are from us, dropping bombs. They don't seem to be fighting back much. Not much tracer fire. But probably there's action for hundreds of miles. We can only see what the reporter can see and hear out his hotel window."

"It looks like fireworks," said Nicky. Nicholas was stuffed with chocolate cookies, his little chest was covered with crumbs and his fingers were sticky with white sugary filling. Licking each finger one by one, Nicholas stood up in the line of his father's vision, blocking the television screen. "Is Mommy dead now?" said Nicholas casually.

There was something so horrifying about little kids. The way they went straight to the point. The sober, calm way they attacked the real nightmare. *Is Mommy dead now?*

"No!" said Dad. "Nobody's dead."

But of course somebody had to be dead. You couldn't fill a sky all these hours with bombs and not have some of them drop on people. That was the point, after all.

"Nobody's dead," repeated their father, and he took Nicky on his lap, as if about to sing a lullabye, *go to sleep, nobody's dead.*

Laura thought of Arab families lying in bed in

Baghdad. They didn't have to watch on TV. They could look out the window.

No, they'd be in their air-raid shelters. Did they have those in Iraq?

She remembered one military briefing where the officers repeated several times that "only military targets would be bombed, not civilian."

Civilian, thought Laura. Mothers and babies and kitchen sinks, gardens and backyards and aunts.

She looked around their TV room. Two doorways opened off it, the larger one into the kitchen, the smaller one into the back porch. It had an old stuffed corduroy couch good for jumping on. Two comfy armchairs, a low scarred wooden table on which they stuck their drinks and snacks. Velvet floor pillows. One large window filled with their mother's hanging plants. It was a homey, beat-up kind of room.

Laura and Langan and Nicholas had spent their lives in this room.

What if a bomb dropped on this room?

What if a bomb dropped on Mommy and she never came home? What if she was fueling some vehicle and something went wrong and there was an explosion? What if Saddam Hussein ordered chemical bombs dropped and Mommy was too slow getting her gas mask on?

On and on and on they watched the television, and the sparkling white dots of explosions in the sky, listening to the sounds from a microphone the American reporter hung out the window of his Baghdad hotel. Flipping channels. Every channel had its experts.

For a moment the screen went black, then checkered, and then the picture disappeared.

"Iraq did that," said Nicholas. "They're here now." He looked up, expecting a missile through the ceiling.

"No, it's just the cable," said their father. "The war is thousands of miles away. Farther away than it takes to drive to see Grandma and Grandpa. There's a whole ocean between us." They kept a globe on top of the television for getting themselves straight on war geography. Dad showed Nicholas the ocean. "Nobody can reach us here, honey," said his father.

"I don't get to shoot?" said Nicholas sadly.

"Only Mom gets to shoot," said Langan.

"Mom is pumping gas," said Nicholas. "She told me so. She said the rifle was just for decoration."

Everybody agreed with Nicholas that Mom's rifle was just for decoration.

But after that nobody had much to say.

At eleven forty-five, Langan said, "I've had enough. I've got school tomorrow. I'm starting electronics. I gotta get some sleep." He walked away as if they had been watching nothing more than the rerun of a sitcom.

Langan—who had fought the whole concept of bedtime since he was Nicky's age? Going to sleep because he had school the next morning? Langan who hated school? Even Wash?

When the war Langan had yearned for had begun?

When Mom was there, her fate unknown?

Nicholas was asleep on the floor with his cheek against the Legos. It looked extremely uncomfortable. Laura stepped over him and walked barefoot after Langan.

Her brother was in the hall, dimly visible in the light coming down the stairway.

He was weeping.

He did not look fourteen, but old; old as Dad; old as war.

He wiped his cheeks dry on his sleeve without seeing her and mounted the stairs numbly, like a cripple.

Laura stepped over Nicholas again and sat back down next to her father. "Daddy?"

"Yes, honey."

"Where do you really think Mom is?"

"I don't know. I don't think we're going to know."

"Near the front?"

"Guess that's where they need most of the fuel," he said. Tears laced his cheeks. The wild exuberance of two hours ago was gone. After a minute he dried his tears with his sleeve. So exactly like

Langan that it was spooky. Had Dad known that his son needed to weep in private for a moment?

It was Laura who wept easily, and often on purpose, because crying made her feel better. But no tears came tonight. Instead a kind of lurching was taking place in her chest, a heart displaced, lungs crowded, guts churning.

Her father took Laura's hand and held it between both of his. "This is it, baby doll. Air war has started and Mommy's there."

CHAPTER TEN

Laura went to bed at one-thirty and fell asleep instantly. But when she woke up it was not her usual seven-fifteen. Much darker, much earlier. She crept downstairs. Her father had never turned the heat down; it was strange to have the rooms still warm. He was sitting in his recliner, staring at CNN. It was 3:00 A.M.

"Do they usually broadcast all night, Dad?"

"I don't know. I've never looked at CNN at three in the morning."

"Did they broadcast like this during the whole Vietnam war? All night every night and preempt everything else?"

"No. The Vietnam war kind of crept up. It was just part of the news."

"Why did you hate Vietnam, Dad?" She had asked him this a thousand times but he didn't lose patience.

"I didn't know why we were fighting," he said. "And we were the bad guys so often. I hated being the bad guy. I always wanted to be the good guy."

"Are we the good guys here, do you think?"

He nodded slowly, several times. "I think so. I would never abandon Israel. I'd never let Saddam Hussein get nuclear weapons. I'd never want an entire region to fall to a vicious dictator. But the thing is, everybody down there is a vicious dictator. And if Saddam doesn't get nuclear weapons, somebody else will. Syria, probably. But when the president spoke, I felt better. I'd like to think a new world order could rise out of the ashes." Her father knotted his fingers and then separated them, staring at the calluses and wrinkles. "But it never has before."

"They're not showing any ashes on TV."

"The ashes are out of sight in Iraq. But they're there."

"Somebody's house, do you think?"

He shook his head decisively. "They don't care about people's houses. They're going for military targets. Airfields and launchers."

Laura felt better too. If they weren't going to bomb little kids and bedrooms and back porches and kitchen tables in Iraq, she wouldn't be bombed either. It would be all this military thing, with their "smart" bombs and their Patriots.

She went back to bed and didn't wake up till morning.

When she got up, Langan was in the shower, and then he was running around the way he always did, as if getting shoes and socks required *Jeopardy*-style genius. She avoided his end of the house and went downstairs. Her father was dressed, Nicholas was dressed, the kitchen was spotless. "Daddy," she said, amazed.

"I stayed up all night," he said. "I had to keep busy or go insane watching all those experts. So I scrubbed the place. I mean right down to the vegetable drawers in the fridge."

She said, "I don't want to go to school today. I want to watch the news."

"Okay."

She blinked. Her father had without argument agreed to let her skip school?

He said, "I'm taking Nicholas to day care and I'll be back. I called in sick. Langan's going to school, he doesn't want to miss the first day of electronics."

Laura could not imagine why Langan was going to school when a war was playing. She said, "Don't you want to watch it?"

"They'll rerun the good parts tonight," said

Langan, "but I don't want to miss any of electronics."

Laura felt that she knew nothing about her brother at all.

"Drop me at the grocery on the way to day care," Laura told her father. "I'll stock up so we can get through the day."

Her father nodded. "Get food to eat in front of the TV," he said.

It was like a suction cup.

They were attached to the television screen.

Laura hated to leave the room. The two of them made forays into the rest of the house for supplies: quick bathroom runs, speedy cold-drink journeys.

They lived silently, fascinated, in front of the television, following the war.

We're war groupies, thought Laura. Like rock-star groupies.

She and her father watched television virtually nonstop for thirty-six hours. Friday morning she went back to school and Dad went to work.

Watching so much news had made her stiff and splintery, like kindling. She tried to fold back into the classroom, pliable and soft like the rest, but it did not happen. She was rigid and slightly out of breath.

If Mom is killed, she thought, they will send a car to get Dad. Dad will come here to get me. The principal will call me out of class and tell me what she knows, which will be nothing.

She did not want to be laughing or having fun if Mom was getting killed during it.

But in third-period history, Bobby George did this hysterically funny takeoff on newsmen getting stuck in their gas masks, and Laura was giggling as hard as anybody else. She didn't think about Mom again until lunch, when she realized she had forgotten to bring either sandwich or money.

Kerry sighed heavily and lent her two dollars. "Get with the program, Laura," she said, meaning—I'm going to be understanding one last time and then, forget it. Starve.

Laura even took a vegetable, carrots that had been cooked for hours and were soft as baby puree, puddled in fake butter. She couldn't bring herself to eat it but at least nutrition was on her plate. Somehow she felt as if she were contributing, because if Mom knew that Laura was thinking about vegetables, Mom would be happy and the war would go better.

Saturday morning Langan was the first up. He moseyed down to the kitchen, putting food ahead of war, and his feet stuck to the linoleum. Nicky's popsicle had dripped last night and Langan distinctly remembered that everybody had chosen to walk around the mess instead of mop it up.

Not once in his life had Langan consciously chosen to be responsible. He hated responsibility. Responsibility gave him a rash.

But he knew something. Laura was going to go only so far in shouldering the house and then she was going to stop. Dad was going to last only so long and then he was going to freak.

So there was slack.

And it was his.

Langan stared at the kitchen floor, sticky and disgusting.

He stood there for a long, long time and then he got the mop.

God, I'd rather have a gun, he prayed.

I gave you a mop, said God.

Langan almost heard him. He even almost looked up.

"Get a grip," said Langan out loud. "It's a mop, not the word of God."

Nobody noticed the clean floor. He didn't even get any credit, let alone any teasing.

That's what this war is going to be, he thought. We're not going to get any credit.

January 21 . . . Peter Jennings said, "The war has now been waged for five days."

Laura stared at the television screen. Five days? That was all? It felt like several months. It felt as if she and these television people had spent their lives in this little room, with the wood stove either too hot or too cold, and supper on trays, and a million Legos on the floor.

It was Martin Luther King Day. Laura tried to make sense of that. Her father had very little use for that holiday, but her mother loved it. She had enough African-American friends through the Guard that she was no longer the racist of her upbringing.

So much for peace. So much for nonviolence, thought Laura. Martin Luther King's nothing now but a day off from school.

Another hero had been added to the family list. General Schwartzkopf. You just looked at him and knew you were in good hands. Laura wondered if Mommy had ever met General Schwartzkopf.

She felt that Martin Luther King would not like it that his holiday was spent thinking about generals and war.

Snow fell.

Langan was screaming with delight; at last he would get rich on driveways. But the snow tapered off early, and he had only two to clear, heavily shaded drives where the snow did not melt off by noon.

Their father did not have a vacation day. Not being a Martin Luther King fan, he did not mind.

Laura knew she should make a special dinner, since she was home; sweep around the wood stove where the chips and bark made such a mess. She should pick up in Nicholas's room and change everybody's sheets.

But she didn't.

She sat watching CNN forever and ever. Somehow they never really said anything new, and yet it remained fascinating, and she felt no need to move. When her father and Nicholas got home, they took their places before the screen as if they had been born there. Her father controlled the remote. His impatience and exhaustion showed. He switched continually among the stations as if thinking that he could speed up the war that way.

"It's supposed to be so hot out here," wrote their mother, "temperatures to fry an egg on the palm of your hand, but it's freezing! Thank God for these big thick parkas. Yesterday Starr and I were so cold we got in bed together. Send me long underwear and wool mittens."

"Why isn't she writing about the war?" said Langan.

"She wrote this before the shooting started. Anyway, she can't write about the war," said their father. "It's forbidden. They'd censor it."

"Censor my mother's letters?" said Laura. Laura was outraged.

"What if some Iraqi opened the letter and figured out where she was and what she was doing?"

157

"Big deal," said Laura impatiently. "They're out on the flat sand in the bright sun. All the Iraqis have to do is fly over and look at where she is and what she's doing."

"Laura, you're such a dope," said her four-year-old brother. "We would shoot them out of the sky before they could look out of their plane."

They added words to their vocabularies. Who had ever heard of a "sortie" before? Now it was a word they used more than "milk" or "pizza."

Sortie. The trip out taken by the bombers, the reconnaissance and photography planes.

"Ten thousand sorties?" echoed Langan when the general giving the briefing finished speaking.

"Day before yesterday it was six thousand, remember?"

"And by evening it was seven thousand."

"That's a lot of fuel," said Laura.

They looked at each other.

Langan said, "I changed the sheets."

"Big deal," she said, but it was, and choked her throat. "Now tell me you even washed them."

"I washed them."

"God bless America. With detergent? And water?"

"And then," said Langan, "I made the beds again."

Laura fell to her knees. "I'm too weak to stand," she said. "Langan Herrick makes beds? Call the media."

CHAPTER ELEVEN

The Herricks had always thrown a Super Bowl party, but this year's Super Bowl came after ten days of Gulf War. Tag had no wife, no hostess, nobody to plan with.

The war had brought a double pounding in every heart: a surge of patriotism, but a fall of fear . . . the specter of death and mutilation, body bags and blindness, tortured captive Americans.

The kickoff for the Super Bowl was 6:18 P.M.

The time difference around the globe meant this was exactly the right moment for the Iraqis to cause their usual nighttime havoc in the Middle East. They liked to drop their Scud missiles in Israel or the Saudi desert around that time. What if right in the middle of the Super Bowl, the television cut away to show Americans dying? Did you want to be having dip and chips, swilling beer, making bets?

The Swazeys, their parents' best friends, said the party was on as always. "No ruining tradition allowed," said Mrs. Swazey, "except we'll bring and organize everything." Nicholas could sleep on the floor in front of the tube the way he did every year. And like always, the men wore sweat suits with team-logo boxer shorts dragged up over the pants. (This year they were half Bills' and half Giants' fans.)

Nicholas of course was not giving up his camo jacket for any dumb football T-shirt. He had asked Santa for a gas mask for Christmas. It was kind of sick, but as Nicky pointed out, mothers in Israel spent every night tucking their kids into gas masks instead of bed. Nicky had been crushed when there was no gas mask under the tree.

Whitney Houston sang the national anthem. She was wonderful. Langan loved how she twirled around the high notes, decorating them, like gospel music.

They wept.

Even Mr. Swazey, who felt tears were for queers, was crying.

"Why's everybody crying?" said Nicholas.

"Because we love America," said one of the other

mothers, hugging him, "but we hate the dying that's coming."

What if all his hugs now are from other people's mothers? thought Laura. What if dying includes Mom?

Her father was hardly aware of the television screen. After a long time, Laura realized he was looking at Rosalys's bridal portrait. Perhaps he's following the plays of their marriage instead of the game, she thought. She wanted to talk with Dad about his wife and his love and his fears, but he would never do that. I've lived with them for fifteen years, she thought, and I know nothing about their marriage. I'm their daughter but their marriage is a foreign country to me.

The halftime show had little kids whose mothers and fathers were in the armed services over in Saudi Arabia. "Why didn't they ask us?" demanded Langan. The children were impossibly beautiful. The whole display was impossibly beautiful.

Laura was jealous. She would have loved to be there with Nicky and Langan, on television, waving at the world with Whitney Houston.

Langan was thinking that the only thing that would make this a better party would be snow falling outside. What was he going to do if Shawnee was right, and winter in Connecticut *was* a wimp, and he never earned any money?

The TV broke suddenly to Peter Jennings.

Langan's gut clenched. Had it happened? Attacks? Scuds?

No. Soldiers, wrapped in army blankets, parkas, and sleeping bags were watching the Super Bowl over there in Saudi Arabia. Drinking soda—booze not being allowed in Saudi Arabia—and full of delight at being able to participate in the Super Bowl even out there in the desert.

"Is Mom watching?" said Nicholas.

"Your mother thinks football is the dumbest sport invented by mankind," said Mrs. Swazey.

Nicky hated half-answers. Laura could not imagine how he was ever going to get through school. "But is Mom watching?" repeated Nicholas irritably.

"Probably," said their father. "Looks like all the troops are."

"Why doesn't she ever telephone us?" said Nicholas.

Somebody made up an answer but they all had the same guess: their mother was not where phone calls could be easily made. Someplace isolated. Someplace dangerous.

". . . so that our loved ones in Saudi Arabia . . ." said the television.

How strange to think of Mom as a "loved one." One of four hundred thousand "loved ones." Americans everywhere were including Laura's own mother in their thoughts and prayers for "loved ones."

The camera flicked briefly to a clip of war protestors.

War protestors made Langan so angry he could hardly breathe. Actually, there were very few protestors. Laura had never seen one except on television from San Francisco, which seemed to Laura as remote as Saudi Arabia.

"Why can't they just shut up?" demanded Langan.

"Because this is America," said his father wearily, "and you're always allowed to talk."

"You shouldn't say things like that, though," said Langan fiercely.

"Like what?" said Laura.

"Anti-American things."

"They're not anti-American, Langan, they're anti-war."

"Same thing," yelled Langan. Langan could not have a discussion. He could only have arguments. Langan was always so hot under the collar it was a wonder he didn't melt.

"It is not the same thing," said Laura in the calm soft voice she knew would just make Langan madder.

"Is too!" bellowed Langan.

This was what their mother referred to as a portable conversation. You could carry it around wherever you went, pick a fight with it even when things were so pleasant that fights seemed impossible.

The Super Bowl was back on and the nine adults in the room were eying Laura and Langan.

Laura felt like starting things. "I don't care who we buy oil from. I'm just as happy to buy oil from Iraq as from Kuwait. I don't know why we're over there."

"What kind of American are you, anyway?" shouted Langan, getting ready to hit her.

"An American who can't figure out what we're dying for!"

"Leave it alone, Laura."

"Why do *I* have to leave it alone? Why doesn't *he* have to leave it alone?" yelled Laura.

Her father pulled her down on the sofa. She flinched. He never glared at her like that. "Because I agree with Langan," said her father.

Laura had gone too far. The room was lined up against her; she could feel their hard eyes and angry hearts. She had ruined the party. It wasn't fair! She wanted these people who wept for a national anthem to—

—to what?

Her mind swirled, like chocolate ripples in ice cream.

If I want war, that means I want Mommy to die. If I don't want Mom to die, that means I don't want war. If I want America to win and be strong, that means I want Mom to be hurt. If I want America to be weak and come home without a fight, that means . . . what does it mean?

What does any of this mean?

Wednesday, January 30, the fourteenth day of the war, Nicholas woke Laura up by jumping on top of her and she responded by trying to smother him in her blankets. It almost worked.

"The ground war has started," said Nicholas happily. "Come look at the news."

Laura froze. "Ground war?"

"Yup. But Mommy's not dead yet."

Laura laughed hysterically. "How do you know?"

"Daddy said."

Laura got out of bed, wrapped herself in her mother's huge white terry cloth robe, whose sash had been lost years ago. She slid her feet into her bunny slippers and ran downstairs. The house was still very cold. She wished they could stop conserving energy and leave the heat up all night. She filled with confused thoughts of oil and war and dead mothers and keeping the heat low. "Daddy?" she said fearfully.

He was sipping coffee, sitting on the ottoman over which he had safety-pinned an old orange-and-white-striped beach towel. Mom would hate that; she cared deeply about colors. Her color this year was cobalt blue: a much deeper, more intense blue than two years ago's dusty blue. But the ottoman was ruined now, because Nicky had tried to hide a spaghetti sauce spill by rubbing it into the upholstery, and Daddy had no solution except the towel.

"It's not ground war yet. They're calling it an incident," said her father. "Several Marines died."

"How many Iraqis?" asked Langan eagerly.

"They're not saying. They're implying serious casualties."

"And Mommy's not dead yet?" said Nicky.

"Don't say it like that or I'll brain you," said Langan.

"I just wanna know!" yelled Nicky.

"Mommy's not going to die, she's not on the front," said their father.

Nicky was scornful. "Tanks are at the front," he said. "They have to have fuel. So there."

Laura's stomach was giving her a hard time. Was it safe to have a glass or orange juice or would she throw it up?

"What is dying, anyhow?" said Nicholas to his sister.

Laura decided to pass. This was why you had parents around, to handle the questions like that. Even Langan decided to take another muffin instead.

Their father said, "Remember the kitten we got last year?"

"I was only three," said Nicky.

"And the kitten was only a few weeks old. Remember how one morning we got up and it wasn't moving anymore?"

"I remember," said Langan. "Nicky kept saying, '*But where did the die part go?*'"

"Where *did* the die part go?" asked Nicky.

"Heaven," said their father, a little too firmly.

"Does Mommy's die part go there too?"

"Mommy," said their father, gritting his teeth, "is not going to die."

Langan said, "Here, Nicky, let's have breakfast. You want Applejacks?"

"I hate Applejacks."

"You want a muffin?"

"I hate muffins."

Langan's patience, never strong, ended. "You want a mouthful of broom handle, then?" he yelled.

Nicky settled for Applejacks.

Laura sat alone on the school bus for two stops, until Johanna and Hope got on. The bus left her neighborhood and doubled back on Main Street. Her town was basically dull, neither beautiful nor quaint. But it was home and Laura loved it. This morning the town crew was putting up American flags. While one worker raised the bucket of the bulldozer, two stood in the bucket, going up. On every second telephone pole, the crew attached a large American flag.

Laura estimated the flags were about twelve feet off the ground.

You could interpret this romantically (high enough for breezes to whip the fabric of the grand old flag) or cynically (high enough to foil vandals).

Laura went with romantic.

Television reigned.

At home they ate, did homework, stayed silent, and sorted laundry in front of the screen.

The big worry was Scud missiles: bomb-carrying—possibly chemical-weapon carrying—weapons that could hurtle out of the sky and destroy so well.

Of course, American Patriots could destroy them right back.

It was just like Nintendo, where suddenly the Scud appeared on some soldier's screen and if he moved fast enough, he could off the Scud with his Patriot and win points.

Nicholas was thrilled with Scuds. He loved the word, for one thing. It had a harsh sound, like swear words he was forbidden to use. "Scud," he'd mutter under his breath, proudly. He regarded it as his job to keep track of Scud incidents: at any time he could give a running list of how many Scuds had hit Israel and how many had hit Saudi Arabia. He had trouble with the concept that Tel Aviv was a city inside the country of Israel and argued for many days that they were different places, but eventually he caught onto the whole map idea and agreed that Tel Aviv could be a piece of Israel. He kept everybody updated on Scud activity and worried all day that he was missing Scud action.

They had a terrific dinner that night: Dad came home with a dozen of those white cardboard boxes only Chinese restaurants use. Everybody dove in, sampling and snacking and happy. There was enough fried rice to go around, and the sweet and sour didn't run out before everybody had had a helping.

The nicest thing about Chinese takeout was doing the dishes. There were none.

Dad swept dinner off the table into the garbage and that was that. Nicky got up on the kitchen counter. "Langan, lookit me," he ordered.

Langan looked.

Nicky hurled himself on top of his brother. "You're a Scud!" shouted Nicky. "And I'm a Patriot!" Nicky drummed on Langan's skull. "Explode!" shrieked Nicky.

Langan obligingly exploded, arms, ribs, and screams penetrating the room like shrapnel. He and Nicky ricocheted off several walls before finally dying on the couch. "You got me," whispered Langan, closing his eyes.

"Cause I'm an American Patriot missile," said Nicky, "and you're nothing but a Scud."

Somebody out there, thought Laura Mary Herrick, knows how to choose a name. They had this newly invented missile-taker-outer without a name, see. Back before KTO (Kuwaiti Theater of Operations). What to name the missile-taker-outer? The Elm Tree? The Killer Bee?

No, let's call it a Patriot. Then when we really do have a war, everybody can sit in their living rooms yelling, "Go! Patriots!"

Nicholas leaped up off his brother. "Scud alert in Jerusalem," he muttered, turning up the volume on the TV. "They're putting on their gas masks."

"The kid is a military genius," Langan told Laura happily. "He's probably going to go into the army and be a general by the time he's sixteen, like Alexander the Great."

They listened to the experts discuss the current threat to various theaters of operation. Laura actually saw them that way: like movie theaters, with surgery going on, while the spectators had popcorn and the experts narrated and the soldiers died.

Nicholas squatted on the floor, holding his ankles in his hands and rocking back and forth, soaking up the information, repeating it softly to himself so he wouldn't forget anything.

"He's a real little Scud puppy," said Langan proudly.

"Just what I want in a brother," said Laura gloomily.

CHAPTER TWELVE

"Good morning, ladies and gentlemen. This is the twenty-ninth day of the Gulf War. As of today, we have flown seventy thousand sorties."

Laura stared at the general on television giving the briefing in Saudi Arabia. *Seventy thousand.* Seventy thousand times a plane had taken off and crossed a desert and dropped a bomb on a target. She could not imagine seventy thousand anything: not seventy thousand sugar cubes, or seventy thousand homework papers, or seventy thousand sit-ups.

It was ten in the morning on a Thursday and she was not in school. It was Valentine's Day, which she had forgotten about until she was already well into skipping school.

Dad had left with Nicky, Langan had caught his bus, and Laura, slowly wrapping her hair around electric curlers, had decided she had better things to do than go to school.

Last night's news haunted her. Her hands trembled brushing her hair. An Iraqi military installation hit by American bombers had turned out to be an air-raid shelter. Hundreds of women and children had been burned to a crisp. Mutilated bodies were carried out of a hideous cement hole in the ground, and American camera crews in Baghdad filmed it.

One victim loaded on a stretcher, a blanket partially tossed over it, had been meat. It just did not look like a person at all. It looked like an unwrapped selection from the meat counter at the supermarket. And how the cameras circled it, hungry cameras, like starved jungle predators, saliva dripping from the lens.

A Connecticut boy had been killed a few days ago.

It had been an accident—a truck crash, not enemy fire.

The town of his birth held a sort of parade, a sort of celebration. Flags and banners and songs.

"If my mother dies," said Laura out loud, aiming her speech at CNN, "I'm not holding any parade."

She made toast but didn't eat it. She poured coffee but didn't drink it.

"I'm not celebrating, do you hear! If my mother

173

gets burned up or full of holes or buried in the cement, I'm not going to be glad she died, do you hear that!"

The television broadcast on and on, unaware of Laura, its smooth calm face endlessly presenting the same films of the same bombed hole.

Ten-twenty.

Lunch at school would be Valentine's Lunch. The cooks would cut the ham sandwiches with a heart cutter; the cake for dessert would be iced in white with red candy hearts. Kids would be tossing valentines across the tables like Frisbees.

Daddy knows I skipped school once, the first day of the war, but he doesn't know this time. If Mom were home, she'd kill me.

Kill. We use that word so carelessly. *You eat my share of the dessert and I'll kill you, Langan. Touch my stereo and I'll kill you, Nicky.* Now I know what "kill" is. It's dead. Horrible dead, like the children in the bomb shelter and the soldier in the truck crash.

I have to go to school. I can't cut like this.

She could not use her mother as an excuse. If she said, "I was upset about my mother," they'd have her in counseling. They were so eager to counsel Laura; they had a whole staff lined up for just this. No way. She was not going outside the family. Daddy didn't want her to.

Which made all other excuses tumble uselessly to

the ground. Because if she said, "I had to dress Nicky and find Langan's safety glasses," they'd say understandingly, "Of course, darling, you're doing your mother's job now, and of course you're ambivalent and upset, come inside and we'll counsel you."

So Laura walked to the convenience store, where she bought a bunch of valentines. When she finally got to school, she said calmly to the office secretary, "I didn't have my valentines ready so I skipped. I know I get a detention. I'll be there after school."

But the secretary buzzed the principal and the principal came out, oozing love and protection and kindness. "Laura, honey, instead of detention, let's you and me have a talk."

Let's not.

"It's upsetting to have your mother in Saudi Arabia and have to take over her role, isn't it, Laura?"

"I'm not taking over her role," said Laura. "We've divided everything up evenly and everybody's pulling his weight."

"Laura, I sense a new anger in you," said the principal, "and I think we should talk."

I want to seethe all by myself, thank you.

"It's not good to let things build up," said the principal.

After twenty minutes of the principal being understanding, and Laura being silent, the result was a phone call to Dad to tell him that Laura needed counseling because she didn't want counseling.

"I told you I didn't want us going to these counseling things," said her father at dinner.

"I didn't go; they took me. I was like their prisoner of war."

"Speaking of prisoners of war," said Langan, taking the largest pizza triangle, "what do you think the Iraqis are doing to that American woman they captured? Raping her?"

"Langan," said Dad dangerously.

"I wish we could watch *Wheel of Fortune*," said Laura. *Wheel of Fortune* kept getting preempted for special war coverage.

"What is rape?" said Nicholas, of course.

Laura and Langan both tried leaving the room, but Daddy was quicker.

The three of them were wedged in the doorway, trying to escape defining rape. Nicholas, however, forgot the question. Pizza had been left unguarded, and he used the time to eat the good stuff off their slices.

Pizza again. What a contrast to Kerry's house. Laura had stopped in there after school. Kerry's house was so full of motherhood that Laura had wanted to sob. It was tidier, actually warmer, because the stove was on. It smelled good, things were lined up neatly, and brownies were coming out of the oven. A chicken pot pie—not from a store—

was ready to slide in as soon as the brownies came out. The piecrust had little piecrust leaves all around the rim.

Her mother cooked like that when there was time. She would have seen that crust on the cover of *Family Circle*, cut it out, and magneted it to the refrigerator. She would have sung to herself, songs without words or tunes, just hummy noises, while she cut out the crust.

Tag had dated Rosalys since ninth grade, and married her at twenty-two. Laura was born the next year. Tag had literally spent his life with Rosalys.

If I miss Mommy, thought Laura, Daddy must *really* miss her. "Why don't you go out tonight?" said Laura.

"With who? You want me to have a date, maybe?"

"Dad," said Langan, who was much more scared of divorce than his sister.

"He's joking," said Laura to her brother. "You can have dinner at the Mexican Hat," she offered, "you love it there. And *Dances with Wolves* is still playing at the movies. You can go see that."

Dad glared. "Why would I want to go to a restaurant alone? And see a movie by myself? Which reminds me," he added, although nothing had been said to remind him, "Mom wants to know what on earth is this nonsense about an eight-hundred-dollar snow thrower?"

He waved a letter at Langan.

"Aw right, who told?" said Langan.

"What'd you do it for if you're not proud of it?" said Laura, proving who told.

"It's gonna snow," said Langan, gritting his teeth. "I'm gonna earn the money. Don't push me. It's gonna be fine."

"Right," muttered Laura. "Daddy, if Langan gets to charge eight hundred dollars on your Sears card, so do I."

"Stop bickering!" yelled Dad. He tilted so far back in his chair he was practically horizontal. "It takes two, that's all I can say. You have to trade back and forth. There is no way on earth for a single parent to stay sane."

"Well, then, Daddy," said Nicholas, with the horrifying practicality of the very young, "let's get another mother."

They stared at him.

"Jason's mommy isn't married, Daddy. She's a divorce. Let's have Jason's mommy instead."

Laura would not have known how to predict her father's reaction to this, but she did not expect what happened. Their father simply got up from the table, got his car keys, walked out of the house, and drove away.

Langan and Laura were terrified. Laura gave Nicholas a calm and complete explanation of why this was not possible, why it was disloyal and sick

178

even to have thought of such a thing. Langan just said if Nicholas ever said that again, he'd have such a split lip they could grow corn in the trench.

Nicholas cried and said he wanted a mommy.

The evening went on.

They put Nicholas to bed.

They did their homework.

Their father hadn't come back yet.

"He's probably out finding another wife," said Langan.

Laura burst into tears.

"He is not," said her brother quickly. "I'm just being a jerk, okay?"

"Where is he?" screamed Laura.

Langan shrugged, though his private guess was a bar somewhere that Dad could count on being with men. No kids. No pressure.

He and Laura got ready for bed at their usual time. Langan tiptoed into her room. "What'll we do if he doesn't come home?"

"He'll be home," said Laura. "Go to bed."

But, she thought, how do we get Nicholas to day care? How do we do anything?

Far into the night, she woke up shuddering, nightmares of flaming oil ditches in her brain: napalm and hideous evil wounds, and her mother's skin and hair on fire. She was afraid to get up and see if Dad was home. Because what if he wasn't?

In the morning Dad was there, making breakfast, looking terribly tired and worn.

"Daddy," said Laura.

He closed his eyes, as though if one more person said one more thing to him, he'd explode.

"I don't care how lousy you feel," said Laura Herrick, her own voice harsh and final. "We feel just as lousy and we didn't run off without a word. So don't do it again."

He looked at her in a sort of astonishment. I'm a woman facing him, she thought; he expected a little girl.

"You sound like your mother," he said.

She kept glaring at him.

"You glare like your mother," he added.

"If she could drive like Mom," said Langan, coming into the kitchen with them, "and if she had a car like Mom, we'd be fine when you play exit. But she's only fifteen. We have another year before that happens."

"Oh, that's all you need, huh? Transportation?" Their father managed a feeble laugh, so they laughed together, and although it was strained, it was real, and Langan, who had thought he could never go to school again, lest his family split behind him, was jelly-kneed with relief.

"Al," said Mr. Grekula. "Something wrong?"

"My name is Langan," he said quietly. He would

never tell them what was wrong. He would never tell them that he was more afraid of divorce than of war.

Shawnee, who weighed twice what Langan did, stood up. She was shaped rather like a set of torpedoes mounted on a vertical ship. Langan was overwhelmed by her. There was so *much* of her. When she folded her arms across her vast chest, he felt as if he were trying to face down an aircraft carrier.

"Hey, honkey."

"Yeah?" said Langan.

"Answer the man. You all right?" Shawnee was not a girl to dis with. But he had to, anyway.

"That first woman missing in action," Langan said finally. "Scared us."

"She gonna be all right," said Shawnee gently, meaning his mother, not the MIA. For the first time, the condensed slang used by black kids did not annoy Langan. It was direct, it worked, and he needed it. "She *your* mama," pointed out Shawnee. "She be brave."

I am brave, thought Langan. Laura and I have been braver than Dad. We've hung on tighter. But maybe that isn't fair. I don't have a family to support and a job at risk. Maybe Dad's been the bravest of all but we can't see. He did come home during the night. Just when you think you can't count on a person, you can count on him.

Somebody put on the radio.

Mr. Grekula said nothing. He didn't teach and he didn't quiz Langan.

Shawnee began dancing. After a while, Langan joined her. And then they were all dancing. The room was rocking with music that somebody turned up louder and louder and louder.

But it seemed to Langan that they had gone far beyond rock and roll. They were dancing to something adult and yet primitive. They were dancing for the safety of a soldier and the fear of death and the love of a country.

For something stronger than family, or God, or race, or friendship.

Patriotism.

CHAPTER THIRTEEN

Mom had been gone three months.

"It's difficult falling asleep," she wrote. "More than anything else—more than sandy, more than hot by day, cold by night, more than military, more than strange—this place is noisy. The noise never ends. Every engine is so huge, and so loud, and there are so *many* tanks and planes. I hope all of you are doing better. Write and tell me how well you're doing."

Today, at last, they could write and tell how well they were doing.

Daddy had ceased to have trouble running things.

Perhaps waiting for war had made him also wait:

183

wait for the household to fix itself. But action in the Gulf brought action at home. Daddy made lasagna from the recipe on the back of the Ronzoni box. He cooked butterscotch pudding. He laid out Nicky's day-care outfits the night before and stopped at the dime store for new shoelaces when Nicky's broke. He noticed that Langan had grown another inch and had to have new jeans. While they were at the mall, he bought Laura a new sweater and Nicky a wall poster of American flags.

Monday was warm again, blue sky, soft air, nothing like winter. Langan had stopped screaming at the weather, and Dad had stopped mentioning the possible return of the snow thrower. He seemed to feel that if there was no snow, Langan would have learned a good lesson in business planning, and if there was snow, Langan would be able to pay for it after all.

Breakfast worked, they had enough milk, everybody had clean clothes and the right change for lunch money. Cheerleading practice was fun and Langan won a prize in robotics. Dad got home with Nicky, who had slept just the right amount at school and was not cranky. Everybody was in the mood for the chili Dad whipped up and nobody's homework made him or her throw the book into the wood stove.

Bedtime and the single bathroom worked as if they'd synchronized watches. Nicky fell asleep in two minutes and didn't wake up. He hadn't mentioned Mommy once.

We're getting into the swing, thought Laura contentedly. It doesn't matter now that Mom's not here. We're fine.

Langan actually wrote that in his next letter. "We're doing fine now without you, Mom, you can stop werring."

"Wor-ry-ing," spelled Shawnee. "Fix it or she'll worry about school."

Langan fixed it. "How do you spell schedule?" he asked.

She told him. They were in study hall, which both of them loathed, because it meant studying. Didn't teachers understand that half the reason they had come to technical school was to avoid studying?

"We've got everything working, Mom," wrote Langan. "Everybody's schedule is good, Nicky is fine, he doesn't even ask for you anymore."

Shawnee said to him, "You a jerk, you know."

He was more hurt than he cared to admit. "Thanks a lot, Shawnee."

"You think your mama's gonna feel better? You don't think about her no more?"

"Sure. Now she doesn't have to worry that we're falling apart."

"She *wants* to worry about that," said Shawnee.

Langan frowned. "She's my mother," he said, "and I think I know—"

"*I* know," said Shawnee. "Rip up the letter and start over." Her immensely long scarlet fingernails tapped the paper like eagle talons.

"When we were saying good-bye," explained Langan very carefully, because he didn't want to lose his temper with Shawnee (first because he liked her, and second because she could and would pulverize him), "Mom said she wanted us to do fine without her."

"She's lying," said Shawnee.

"Listen," said Langan, getting hot.

"*You* listen," said Shawnee, changing dialects. "Your mother is a lot more scared of being forgotten than being in Saudi Arabia. Who wants to be forgotten? She wants Nicky to do fine but she also wants Nicky to cry for her. She's the *mother*, you turkey. She wants to come home to her *place*. She doesn't want the slot closed while she's gone! Rip up the letter."

"Right," said Langan, ripping.

Ground war would be when General Schwartzkopf actually moved the troops out of Saudi Arabia and into Kuwait. It was still air war except that a few things were also happening on the ground.

The planes were flying an unbelievable number of missions. It was impossible to imagine the sky over which so many jets screamed. The televisions, unfortunately, could film only the boring squares of sand on which the correspondents stood. At least the bombers had cameras in their nose cones, so you could see the smart bombs finding their way into the chosen window of the chosen building of the Iraqi supply dump. Poof! went the building, soundlessly and smokily vanishing.

"Forty thousand missions," whispered Laura. "Wow."

The bombers were not hitting people but only things: bridges, roads, storage areas.

And yet . . . if at each bomb site, just one single soldier stood guard . . . there must be forty thousand dead Iraqis.

And soldiers didn't do anything alone, did they? Didn't they always do things in pairs, or squadrons, or regiments? So wouldn't there have to be many, many more dead men? Even more than forty thousand?

Do I care this much about oil? thought Laura Herrick. Will they stop bombing Mommy if we don't stop bombing them? But we have to bomb them. Everybody's decided that.

An army officer on the television was showing various land mines to his soon-going-into-battle infantrymen. They ranged from the size of tuna cans to hubcaps and that's what they looked like, too.

"This one here," said the officer, waving a hubcap, "you play games with this one and all that's left is red mist."

"What's red mist?" said Nicholas.

"I don't know," said their father rather quickly, "I didn't understand either."

Langan, who had many properties of jerkdom, said, "Dad, obviously it means—"

Laura pinched the back of her brother's neck.

Langan was too dumb to interpret this. He swung around, holding Laura's wrist in a vise meant to break bones, and continued with his interpretation, "Nicky, they step on one of those, and they blow up into so many little tiny pieces of meat and bone that all their buddies are going to see is a spray of blood in the air. There won't be anything to bury. The person who steps on that is going to rain red on the sand."

There was a long terrible silence in which their father closed his eyes, Laura stared at the wall, and Nicholas thought about it.

"Mommy?" said Nicholas at last. "That's what the die part is?"

"No, of course not," said their father. "Mommy is not going to be at the front."

Nicholas said, "Peter Jennings says there is no front."

Laura could not believe her four-year-old brother knew this stuff.

Nicholas said, "Tiny pieces of meat? Like hamburger?"

"I was exaggerating," said Langan, finally catching on. "That wouldn't really happen."

Laura thought that if she could write up a red-mist list, Langan would be first on it.

Nicholas said fearfully, "Daddy?" He climbed up onto his father's lap.

Daddy said, "I'm here, sweetheart. Everything's okay. It's just television."

"But Mommy isn't here," said Nicholas, and they knew that at last he knew. He had understood war and death. It was not going away. It was his mommy, whose T-shirt and pearls were all he had left, being blown up into a red mist.

"I want to call Mommy and tell her I'm not feeling so good," said Nicholas, when the 800 numbers for the armed services appeared on the screen.

"We can't do that," said their father. "That would make Mommy feel bad too."

"I want Mommy to feel bad!" said Nicholas. "I want her to come home! She's been gone long enough!"

"I'll drink to that," he said gloomily.

They kept sorting and folding laundry.

The master-bedroom pile was skimpy. No Mom clothes in it.

No Mom anywhere. Like a rehearsal for Mom's

death. A stage set for a house without a mother ever again.

No tears fell. Instead they suffered from a sort of dry, parched desert of the heart.

Oh, Mommy! thought Laura. We need you! Stay alert.

Chapter Fourteen

The next letter was different. No giggly stories about volleyball, Starr flirting, or taking sand showers.

"I feel I am ready," wrote Rosalys Herrick. "I run things through my mind constantly, making sure I know what I am doing, that I will not forget when I'm scared. I am not so much afraid as very awake. Every inch of me, every brain cell of me, is paying attention. Nothing has ever meant my life before."

Peace proposals had been flying around: the Soviet Union was working hard with Tariq Aziz to put forth proposals that would satisfy both the United Nations coalition (which actually seemed to mean

President Bush) and Iraq (which definitely meant Saddam Hussein).

But Saddam Hussein wouldn't make enough promises to please America. He still thought he could be a bully and win.

President Bush said finally that Saddam had to be out of Kuwait, or starting to leave, by noon on Saturday.

Ground war was coming, sure as seasons and tides.

President Bush's deadline was convenient. They could have a late breakfast in front of the tube and watch the war begin.

There was something very Saturday-morning-cartoon-like about the whole thing. Laura pictured the two leaders standing on the set of a TV western, legs spread, hands ready to draw.

Dad cooked serious food, pancakes and bacon, as if the spectators needed to be well nourished to hold up their end. They sat in front of CNN and heard about the preparedness levels of the Saudi, British, American, and Iraqi armies.

Naturally U.S. troops were the best prepared.

But the U.S. could be there for years, said the experts, while the enemy dug into their sand trenches and shot from their tanks and generally killed thousands of people. They were people whose Allah told them death with honor was a good thing. They yearned for death. They were not like our troops, who had never seen war and were pretty sure they didn't want to.

Noon came and went, and war did not begin, and once again everybody lost interest.

"Let's *do* something!" said Langan, pacing around.

Dad switched through every channel again, as if hoping to find a war between the cartoons. All they got was a list: the war dead as of Saturday morning (U.S. casualties, at least; nobody had the slightest idea about the Iraqis) were:

20 dead

30 missing

9 known prisoners of war

Laura comforted herself that this was nothing. An unfortunate handful. Not her mother.

When Mommy had telephoned them last week, she'd said, "We're good to go." It didn't mean well behaved. It meant ready. Nicholas was saying it all the time now. "I'm good to go," he'd yell, when it was time to leave for school.

Good to go.

They waited and waited. America might be good to go, but nobody went Saturday morning.

The afternoon dragged. They got on each other's nerves.

Daddy suggested a night out. They were so relieved to be turning the TV off and getting away from the house that nobody argued over the choices: Mexican food, the movie *White Fang* (because the rating meant Nicky could see it), and ice-cream sundaes afterward.

Dinner and movie were fine, and afterward, Laura savored a hot butterscotch sundae, letting the vanilla puddle at the bottom of the big glass bowl and drinking it. Nicholas had an M&M sundae, and Daddy didn't make him wipe his mouth afterward. Oh, well, it was Daddy's upholstery getting chocolate-stained. Laura couldn't stir herself to do the napkin work herself.

They got in the door at 9:57 and Langan went straight to the TV. Laura went upstairs to brush her teeth. Her father came into the bathroom with her, starting Nicky's bath, stirring the bubble crystals that were the only thing that made Nicky willing to sit down in water.

"Dad!" Langan yelled. "Laura! Ground war has started!"

"No," said Laura, rather conversationally, rejecting the possibility.

"Hurry up!" yelled Langan.

"Why?" said Laura. "Is the war going to be over in sixty seconds?"

"Shut up, Laura," yelled Langan.

"Stop talking!" screamed Nicholas. "I can't hear!"

Laura and her father arrived in the family room. Nicholas was standing in front of the television: he was so small that he was at eye level with the commentators. "Siddown, Nicky," said Langan.

"Shut up!" screamed Nicholas. He was trembling. Sticky and dirty. Spilled orange soda matted his shirt. Popcorn was stuck between his teeth. Marshmallow sauce from his sundae was smeared across the bottom of both sleeves. It was ten o'clock at night, and a little boy who usually went to bed at seven-thirty was exhausted and cranky.

"Mommy!" screamed Nicholas, getting even closer to the screen. He looked as if he would try to climb in there and find her himself.

There were no films of this supposed ground war. Just talk. Commentators. Retired admirals. United Nations correspondents. "Make them shut up!" Nicholas screamed at the TV. TV was so real to him he talked to it, and not to his family. "I want to see Mommy! I want to see what's going on!" He grabbed the remote and stabbed at the channel buttons, ripping past ABC, NBC, CBS, and CNN. He transferred his stickiness to everything he touched.

Langan said, "Stand still, you little Scud puppy." He peeled his little brother's clothes off. In a cold house, wearing only his underpants and socks, four-year-old Nicholas shivered in front of a television, trying to see his mother. Once he even stood at an angle to the screen, as if hoping to see behind the expert and catch a glimpse of Mommy.

"Twenty minutes till the military briefing," said

their father quietly. "Let's have a bath while we're waiting, Nicholas."

"No!"

"Yes."

"Eat Scuds!" screamed Nicky, eyes blazing, lip jutting, small chest swelling in rebellion.

Their father silently scooped Nicky up and carried him upstairs, wailing and screaming. The howls dwindled to choking hiccupy sobs, and then Nicholas came downstairs alone, bare, draped loosely in an old beach towel. His hair dripped. His eyes were red. His little chest heaved.

Langan knelt. He wrapped Nicky's towel more tightly, making a hood over the squeaky clean hair. Then he stood up, holding Nicky like a baby, rocking slightly, letting Nicky rest his head against his chest and still see the TV. "Nothing's happened yet," Langan assured him.

Secretary of Defense Dick Cheney appeared.

Laura liked his tie. How did you choose the right tie to announce that ground war had begun? To tell the children watching that their mothers or fathers were moving forward in the sand to die?

Basically Cheney told them nothing except that yes, at eight o'clock EST, ground war had begun. They were, he added, suspending military briefings.

"We must assume the enemy is confused about the battlefield," said Cheney. "Even the most innocent-sounding information could endanger the men and women in the operation."

"What's it mean?" whispered Nicky. "What's suspend?"

"It means they're not gonna tell anybody anything because the enemy watches TV too, and they might learn something and use it against us."

Nicky screamed at Cheney, "No! Tell me about my mommy. You Scud! I hate you, you Scud!"

The Secretary of Defense remained calm. He said he could not compromise the security of the situation.

"MOMMY!" screamed Nicholas.

They let him scream. For the second time that night the screams finally dwindled, turned to sobs, to sniffs, and then at last Nicholas slept in his brother's arms. Langan carried him to his room, lay down on the unmade bed, and slowly eased him onto the sheets without waking him. He took away the damp towel. Tucked the blankets in. After a moment's thought he added another blanket to make up for no pajamas.

He went back downstairs.

Of course there was no new news. Just old news.

That's what a lack of briefing meant: we're silent, guys. Guess. Wonder. Worry.

"Thank you, son," said his father, meaning Nicholas.

"No problem," said Langan, and it hadn't been. Boy, am I mature these days, thought Langan.

The wild triumphant excitement of the beginning of the air war touched none of them this time. They were as tired as Nicky. Laura wanted desperately to get some sleep, but didn't say so. For her mother's sake, she had at least to see the news.

It was eleven-thirty on Saturday night.

If Mommy was at war, she'd been at it three and a half hours.

Was she alert enough?

Was she awake and aware?

"Stay alert, Mommy," whispered Laura.

"The world needs more lerts," agreed Langan. He put his arm around his sister. The touch unglued her. She began to weep convulsively. Daddy put his arm around them both and for a few moments Langan tolerated all that emotion. Then he sat on the floor, amid the Legos, safe from physical affection.

"The first twenty-four hours," said a guest admiral, "are the most critical."

"I can't stay awake that long," said Laura.

"Let's sleep in shifts," said Langan. "We can wake each other up if there's any news."

They agreed. Laura went to bed first. Langan and his father collected pillows and blankets. Langan took the couch; his father, the recliner.

They waited.

An Englishman warned that if an air battle lasted thirty-eight days, so would a land battle. He said to expect chemical weapons right away.

It's seven-thirty in the morning where Mom is, thought Langan. Is she having breakfast or bullets?

CHAPTER FIFTEEN

Langan slept quite easily. He awoke to a still-chattering television. Nothing had happened during the night, or at least nothing anybody was going to tell. Langan stumbled off the couch and made a pot of coffee.

He felt good. It had begun, and that was a relief more than a worry. The waiting had been the kill.

Laura came down and had a cup of coffee too. Dad slept on.

At 9 A.M. General Schwartzkopf gave a briefing. "At zero four hundred hours locally," he began.

Langan loved that. Zero four hundred hours. He wanted to talk that way. No wonder people became generals.

General Schwartzkopf said that friendly casualties were "remarkably light." Langan liked that phrase too. Remarkably light. Dead soldiers, but not enough to worry about. Light ones.

Laura couldn't get used to the way the army used the word "friendly." The general meant "wounded people on our side" but it sounded as if the wounds themselves were friendly: a nice friendly bullet hole in your side, a nice friendly chemical burn.

But General Schwartzkopf said that so far, any chemical weapon reports were bogus.

"Bogus," repeated Nicky softly, eating dry Rice Krispies. Laura had not heard him come in. "Want me to pour your milk?" asked Laura.

Silently he held out his bowl for milk.

We gather in front of the TV news the way ancient people used to gather in front of their chieftain, thought Laura, or their hearth fire.

She pictured the Iraqis gathering before Saddam Hussein like that, obedient to his every lie.

It did not sound from the list of units going into Kuwait as if Mommy was anywhere around. They wouldn't use reserves on day one, they'd use regular army. Mom would be backup.

We're home safe, thought Laura. We're there, we're good to go.

She began laughing silently. It's okay, Mom, she thought, just sit tight a little longer, stay alert, the world needs more lerts, then you can come home.

She decided to make cinnamon toast and began hunting down the cinnamon.

General Schwartzkopf was asked how exactly he planned to defeat the Iraqis and take Kuwait City.

"Around—over—through—on top—whatever it takes," replied the general, in a tough warlike way, and the three men in Laura's family were happy.

By Sunday night, Americans and allies were virtually sailing across the desert. The mines that could turn American soldiers to red mist—they seemed to be doing no damage. The Iraqi Republican Guard that was supposed to be so dangerous—they seemed to have vanished. The Iraqi courage—it was invisible. Friendly casualities remained remarkably light.

Laura patted the letter from her mother that she kept in her jeans pocket: the one her mother had written when she was thinking about death. *If I do not come home, honey, if I die here, I want you to be brave and not worry about me. I want to bring you up, and see you grow, and love you every minute of it. But I am willing to die for my country. I am a soldier and I want you to be proud of me whatever happens.*

I'm proud, Mom, thought Laura Herrick. But it looks okay. It looks as if we can breathe again.

Laura herself felt remarkably light.

By Monday morning, when they were dressing for school and work, it was clear from the TV reports that the war was going incredibly well for the allies.

In thirty-six hours, only four people had been killed, and twenty hurt.

Only four people! thought Laura. That doesn't even count. You wouldn't even notice four people. Why, that many probably would have been in car accidents back here anyway. Four! Nothing!

Ten thousand prisoners had been taken, or had surrendered. The TV showed long amazing lines of Iraqi soldiers trudging toward wherever they would be locked up. Ten thousand.

Laura stopped worrying. America knew what it was doing, let them do it. Around, over, through, on top, whatever it takes, they knew how. Mom would come home, and Laura had had enough of this war frenzy, she had school to do. She had Kenny to flirt with and Jan to annoy. She had songs to sing and cheers to cheer. She had papers to pass in and notes to take. She had lipstick to try and sweaters to trade.

Langan was disappointed. No fair, he thought. It's no fun when the other side gives up.

I wanted a real war. I wanted us to smash our way through and be heroes.

This is a cakewalk. I feel like calling up Saddam Hussein and yelling, "At least put up some fight, buster! After all your noise, I expected a better show than this!"

He sat silently on the school bus during the long ride to the regional high school. Around him everybody smoked like mad; he didn't know a single kid at Wash who didn't smoke. People ate their bag lunches for breakfast and tossed a Pepsi can around, sipping in turns without spilling a drop.

"Hardly any friendly casualties," said one of the kids.

"The whole thing's a nonevent," said another.

I wanted a real show too, thought Langan. We got an air show on television. I wanted a ground show, too.

He had wanted a better war.

Langan held his breath a moment, horrified by his thoughts, knowing he would never tell anybody, not even the people he knew would agree.

He got off the school bus and Astle saw him, and Shawnee, and they yelled hi and waited for him, and Langan Herrick forgot the war.

He jogged over. Shawnee said, "Lacy's got a crush on you."

"Lacy?" Lacy was a cute girl who wanted to do computer-aided drafting. She was small and pixieish, with looks that reminded him oddly of his grandmother: delicate and ivory. He was thrilled that Lacy might like him. Terrified that he was supposed to act on it. Worried that Shawnee was teasing him. Afraid Astle was waiting for him to be a man, whatever that meant, however you did that at age fourteen with a girl named Lacy.

"Lacy," agreed Shawnee. She was teasing, he knew by her immense grin. But whether she was telling the truth as well, he did not know.

He said to Astle, "Is Shawnee trustworthy?"

Astle laughed. "This is your war, man."

Langan grinned. He put his arm around Shawnee. She was so immense he hardly reached the middle of her back. They walked down the hall together.

The war is a bummer, thought Langan, but that's what war is supposed to be. I've got two new friends and that's what counts.

Nicholas made a card for his mother. He folded a piece of construction paper in half. It was not easy. It would not lie flat. At last he managed it. Carefully he copied the words TO MOMMY on the front. Exhausted, he handed it to his teacher. She followed his pencil lines with a white worm of glue and gave it back. Nicholas chose silver and blue glitter this time and dropped handfuls of it on his red paper.

They stood it up to dry.

Nicholas ran out to play. Daddy had said the war was a snap, no problem, Mommy'd be calling soon, not to worry. And Daddy clearly was not worrying, for he had laughed, and chatted with the teachers, and wasted time.

Nicholas was first on the swings and his favorite playground teacher was there to push. Nicholas swung and swung, and thought of nothing but going higher, and getting closer to the sky.

The ground war lasted four days.

Four.

Laura could not understand it. How could this have happened, when they expected such horror from Saddam Hussein? Was this even a real war, like World War Two, or the Civil War? Did it count, when it was so short and over so fast and so easily?

"Paper tiger," said one of her teachers. "It's a Chinese phrase, meaning you got incredibly scared of a vicious, enormous, slavering tiger—and here it was just a drawing on paper."

Saddam Hussein had been a paper tiger.

There had been no Mother of Battles. No red mists of young American soldiers. No chemicals; no need for MOPP suits. Iraqi soldiers surrendered so completely that it was stupefying. Five thousand, then ten thousand, then twenty thousand. It was like the number of air sorties: in no time, the numbers were too high to believe.

Surrender stories were so sad. The Iraqis were so hungry, scared, dirty, and tired, they even surrendered to a reporter armed only with a camera. They kissed the feet of the American soldiers who took them.

Langan was utterly repelled by that. He sympathized with the American soldier who quickly backed up, saying, "You don't need to do that." Langan was amazed at the depth of his own pity for the prisoners. He was terribly angry at their leader for not bothering to feed or protect them.

"Cannon fodder," said Mr. Grekula. "Fodder is cattle feed. That's all Saddam's men were to him. Something to feed the enemy."

Nicky did not like it that the prisoners had to sit on the ground with their hands tied: tens of thousands of them. "Are we going to be nice to them?" said Nicky anxiously.

"Yes," said Laura. "Our doctors are fixing them up and our cooks are giving them lunch."

They learned that General Schwartzkopf had moved enough food, supplies, and fuel up to his attack lines to last his troops for sixty days.

Four was all it took.

The logo on the television station changed. No longer WAR IN THE GULF: DESERT STORM, it was now TOWARD PEACE IN THE GULF.

Toward Mom coming home, thought Laura.

The war, which had consumed them for so many months, which had been life and breath, faded.

It was mildly interesting to hear the opinions of the Saudi Arabian ambassador on what would happen next, but only mildly. You didn't have to be an expert to figure out that Iraq had been whipped in minutes. When President Bush said that American troops would begin coming home very soon, Langan actually switched the TV to a non-news channel, and they were amazed to find that regular TV had been going on all this time.

"Regular lives must have been going on, too," said Laura. She could not imagine it. No war in your heart or your household? What would the winter have been like without the war? It seemed to Laura that there had not been *anything* since November except the war, and Mommy gone. And now the war was gone.

Nicky said, "There's nobody left shooting, is there?"

"Hardly anybody," said their father.

"They couldn't still shoot Mommy by accident, could they?"

"I don't think so," said their father. "I'm not worried anyway."

"What if at the very last minute, just as she's calling us up to say good-bye, a Scud hits her?" said Nicky.

There was something horrible about Nicholas, the way he said things out loud. Were all little kids like this, or just Laura's own spooky little brother? Perhaps he was demented.

"A Scud won't hit her," said Daddy.

"It hit that barracks," pointed out Nicholas.

"Twenty-eight American soldiers including two women died."

Laura waited for Daddy to lose his temper. But he didn't. The fever of war worry and war excitement had abated; Daddy was normal.

"You know what let's do?" said Daddy. He swung Nicky into the air over his head and held him up there, nibbling Nicky's belly button.

"Daddy!" shrieked Nicky. "I'm too old for that. Stop that."

"Let's go on a thrill ride," said Daddy. "We haven't taken the Jeep out since Mommy left. We'd better get our thrill rides in, or Mommy will be home and tell us it's not safe."

"I don't see how a woman who went to war can ever tell anybody what they're doing isn't safe," said Langan. Langan thought maybe his mother would let him get a chain saw. A woman who used grenade launchers could not quibble about a chain saw, could she?

"When she gets home," said Daddy, laughing and happy, "she won't be a woman who went to war anymore. She'll be Mommy."

Laura Mary Herrick wondered about that. Was it going to be Mommy who came home? Or Specialist Herrick? Or Rosie? Or Rosalys?

The three men in Laura's family grabbed jackets and headed for the Jeep. "Come on, Laura!" yelled Langan. "Let's have a thrill ride."

That's what the war was, thought Laura. A thrill ride. A television thrill ride. We were more thrilled than most people, and bumped our heads on the roll bar more, because Mommy was there.

She wondered how thrilled Iraq was. It had not been the mother of all battles. It had been a pathetic exercise of Third World versus First. They were the ones who would have to cheer for the losers and bury the dead. Allah be with them, thought Laura, directing her prayer to the name that ought to listen hardest.

She got in the backseat with Nicholas, who complained fiercely that he did not need a car seat any longer, even for thrill rides, he was very grownup, what was Daddy's problem?

"My problem is," said Daddy, strapping Nicky down, "that I love you guys. Wouldn't it be the pits if Mommy made it through the war and we got hurt on a thrill ride?" He kissed his little son, and straightening up, met Laura's eyes. He paused, and then leaned over Nicky, and kissed his daughter. "You fought a good war, kiddo," he said huskily.

"Thanks, Daddy."

"We did the homefront okay, didn't we?" he said.

"With lapses," said Laura.

"She really is just like Mom, isn't she?" said Langan. "Had to point out our shortcomings. Don't kiss me, Dad. Just start the car. Or better yet, let me start it. Let me drive."

Father and son picked up a familiar, portable argument.

Mommy will be home soon, thought Laura. But nothing broke while she was away. We're still a family. There was a war, and we outlasted it.

She said, "I'm the one who's closest to sixteen. If anybody gets to start driving, it's me."

Her father and older brother turned around and looked at Laura.

"Langan got to keep the snow thrower," Laura pointed out.

"Which has nothing to do with anything," Langan said.

"You may back the Jeep out the driveway," said their father to Laura, as graciously as if bestowing a medal of honor.

Laura got into the driver's seat and took the wheel, thinking that for several months she had been there anyway, while they were on the homefront.

"She'll probably wreck it," said Langan, gloomily jealous.

"She'll be fine," said their father.

"Just get going!" yelled Nicky. "You take too long!"

For a moment, Laura could not see anything, her eyes blurred with tears of love for her dumb old bickering family. Then she got hold of herself and showed Langan a thing or two about driving.

ABOUT THE AUTHOR

CAROLINE B. COONEY is the author of many novels for young adults, including *Among Friends*, *The Girl Who Invented Romance*, *Camp Girl-Meets-Boy*, *Camp Reunion*, *Family Reunion*, *Don't Blame the Music*, an ALA Best Book for Young Adults, *The Face on the Milk Carton*, and *Twenty Pageants Later*. She lives in Westbrook, Connecticut.

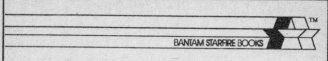